TRIPHAMMER

Dan McCall

TRIPHAMMER

A MORGAN ENTREKIN BOOK
THE ATLANTIC MONTHLY PRESS
NEW YORK
·

Published simultaneously in Canada
Printed in the United States of America
FIRST EDITION

Library of Congress Cataloging-in-Publication Data

McCall, Dan.
    Triphammer / by Dan McCall.
    ISBN 0-87113-333-4
    I. Title.
    PS3563.C334T75   1989   89-6542   813'.54—dc20

The Atlantic Monthly Press
19 Union Square West
New York, NY 10003

FIRST PRINTING

FOR MELISSA BANK

TRIPHAMMER

It's ten below out there, snow blowing around like a bastard, when we receive a call from a father concerned about his twelve-year-old son. The boy always comes home from school after sports practice, promptly at five-thirty, and now here it is eight o'clock and no sign of him. The boy's customary route is through a mile of woods, and the father says maybe he's fallen and broken his ankle and can't get up—in this weather he could freeze to death.

So I take down a description of the boy, his height and weight and color of hair, what he was wearing (yellow ski parka), the names of his friends, teachers' names. I tell the father I'll be back in touch. When I check with the friends, they tell me the boy said he wasn't going to sports practice, said he had something else to do. The last-period teacher says the boy had been in class and everything seemed fine. The sports coach says the boy is a hard worker. I go out, get in a patrol car, and cover the roadways in the immediate area. I check the hangouts where the kids go after school. I return to the station, call the father, and tell him I have been unable to locate his son. Then I contact the chief at home. He does his usual hemming and hawing, finally decides to organize a search party.

We gather all the policemen we can find and a dozen volunteer firemen. By ten o'clock we have got everybody assembled, and we comb the wooded area. It's about a mile long and a quarter mile wide—heavy underbrush, gullies, cricks, culverts under the roads. We walk slowly, with flashlights, arm's length apart, covering every inch of that particular area. The process of searching is pretty quiet; what you hear is the men's low voices and the *crunch, crunch* of boots on the crusted snow and ice, all over the hillside. By 1:00 A.M. the bitter cold takes its toll—you can hardly breathe; you reach a point of agony just trying to make yourself move. The boy's father is with us every step of the way. I have been rather dubious of finding the boy. I think maybe he's just mad at his parents and has gone to somebody's house and will show up in the morning. It's Friday night, kids tend to wander on the weekend. Besides, his friends said he told them he had something to do. Kids have their schemes and little plans. So we call off the search, everybody goes home to get warm. Our night man continues to circle the area. We notify other agencies in the hope that they'll find him wandering around the Commons or stopping in at an all-night restaurant.

The usual procedure is to wait twenty-four hours before putting out a missing person report. You don't want to tie up the teletype unless you have reason to believe a crime has been committed. Older people are not required to check in with anybody; they can just be out of town for the day. To be missing is not a crime. If you have a case of custodial interference, where one of the divorced parents snatches a child, it puts things into a different light immediately. You want to apprehend the person before he or she gets out of state. In that event you need paperwork to show total custody. But none of that stuff applies here, the father had expected his son home any minute. And I suspect the boy's hiding out somewhere. In my mind I see him walking home at sun-up; my imagination pictures him in that yellow ski parka, trudging along the street in the dawn.

That, however, is not the case. When I return to work at 7:00 A.M. there is still no sign of him. I call the parents, and the father is extremely agitated. I try to reassure him. Hours go by, and I am in and out of the station, doing the dink work that we always have to do when the weather is this bad—fender benders, people fall on the ice, pipes freeze and break. Around noon we get a call from one of our officers on patrol; he says maybe we have found our boy. A pedestrian has spied a body at the bottom of Buttermilk Falls. The chief and I take a cruiser down there pretty fast.

When we get out on the bridge and look down over the side, my heart skips a beat. At the deepest point of the gorge, two hundred feet down there, is the yellow parka. The body looks extremely small.

You cannot rule out an accident; kids are always playing around the gorge and falling. There is also the possibility of foul play. But we have a problem on our hands—how do we get down there and get him out? There are huge amounts of ice on both sides. We call in a wrecker, send down a body basket. I'm standing around on the bridge in the cold, thinking just how cold the boy must be. Or had been.

Our men go down in little mincing steps and long slides. It takes them a good half hour to arrive at the body. Up here on the bridge the chief and I are not in a good mood. You work this job many years, as I have done, and you still feel the anguish and senselessness of somebody who ends up in the bottom of a gorge.

They have a problem down there. The body is frozen into the ice, partly frozen into it. But eventually they get him out, and into the body bag, and it's slowly raised up on the cable. An ambulance takes it to the morgue on the directions of the medical examiner. During the process of retrieval the chief directs me to respond back to the house and notify the parents. It is really his job, and he knows the family. Of course it is not a task you relish at all. You never want to make notifications, and this is particularly distressful because of the age of the child involved. Your mind jumps in right away and asks you what is the reason he ended up down there. Was it on purpose or not on purpose? So I drive very slowly, trying to collect my thoughts and figure which way to approach the problem. I haven't the foggiest notion of how to tell them. I mull things over, trying to find the easiest way. Without meaning to, you can be cruel. I get several very elegant speeches prepared. When I arrive at the address, the driveway is covered with ice. I don't want to tell them and then be stuck down there unable to depart. So I park the cruiser up on the road and inch my way down on foot. It's a big stone mansion—the father is a local attorney, quite successful; he works with the Town Fathers. Big bucks. The house is imposing, like a fortress. But, I think, it could not protect him and his family.

The mother answers the door in her bathrobe. She is a very pretty lady. I say to myself, Gee, she's pretty. I am trying to put off the inevitable, that I have to tell her her son is dead. But by the expression on my face she can see that I am not a bearer of good news. With her arm holding open the storm door she says to me, "You found him."

I nod and say, "Yes, we found him."

A long moment goes by, and she says, "He's dead."

I nod my head again. "Yes."

All is silent for a brief while, and then she looks at me and says, "You'll have to tell his father. I can't do it."

Which throws me into a panic, because I thought that once I told her I'd be done. Actually, what I had pictured was telling the father.

Now she says, "I'll go get him."

I think to myself, *Don't go get him. You tell him.* But I see I will have to go through it once again.

She has me come in. I stamp my feet on the mat, and then I find myself in a spacious living room, very elegantly furnished, with a big fire going in the fireplace. It's full of antiques and Persian rugs. It looks like the kind of All-American Living Room you see on the commercials for Hallmark Hall of Fame Christmas specials. This is the kind of home you place yourself in, sitting in your big chair by the fire, your collie dog snoozing at your feet. There are some toys scattered about, and I can hear children's voices in the back of the house. I stand here self-conscious in the middle of the room.

The father comes in, he's tall, about my height, maybe five years younger, although he's starting to lose his hair. He's partially dressed, a T-shirt and a pair of slacks, leather slippers on his bare feet. He's carrying a can of Pepsi. I call him by name and say, "I have terrible, terrible news to tell you." I lose my nerve again when I watch his hand squeeze the pop can. I have to do it, though, and I tell him straight out: "We found your son"—I see his hand squeezing the pop can—"We found him, and he's dead." The father squeezes the can so hard the Pepsi comes out the opening. His face goes white, and he pulls himself over to a grandfather chair. The Pepsi can is in his left hand, and his right hand goes up to his forehead. He sits down and bows his head and starts to cry. His wife goes over to him and tries to comfort him. The only sounds in the house are those kids in back, playing on Saturday morning.

After a few minutes he composes himself and asks me how it happened. I don't know how it happened. I tell him it's the gorge at Buttermilk Falls, apparently the boy slipped or fell. We talk a little, kind of letting our sentences trail off. His wife sits on the arm of the grandfather chair, her hand going through his thinning hair. The boy, it seems, has had psychological problems over a number of years. They had put him in counseling, and he had undergone therapy in several different areas. He had problems in adjusting socially. The father says, "The other kids made fun of him. He was a loner." Seems he'd rather play with his ant farm than his peers. But he had never threatened suicide. He was just marred. Marred in some fashion. Actually, he seemed to be on the upswing recently. He'd never gone out for sports before. His faithful attendance at practice looked like a turn for the better. If they had had any suspicion he'd do something like this, they would have taken steps and put him into a different kind of counseling. They would have pursued other types of help. Of course, we do not know for sure that it wasn't an accident. As time goes by, I watch the father trying to fix it up in his mind as an accident. A natural move for a parent to make. How could a twelve-year-old have such terrible problems that he would take his own life? Kids of that age often see their difficulties as insurmountable. But how could life seem so devoid of hope that he would be driven to jump off a bridge?

The mother goes to the big bay window and looks out. She says they can furnish us with the doctors' confidential reports, to substantiate what they have been saying. I've been standing the whole time, waiting for them to ask me to sit down. But they are in shock.

The father says to me, "Would you help me tell the girls?"

All I want to do is get out of here, not to be hanging around. But they call the children in. Now I do sit down, on the couch, with these two little girls beside me. They're picture perfect, twins, about eight years old, with their mother's hair and coloring. Since it is Saturday, they're still in their pretty blue jammies. They look frightened; they suspect something because, number one, a policeman is in their living room, and number two, their father is white as a sheet. The girls sit here, like little princesses, and it's all silent. I am waiting for the father to start telling them. One girl tries to make small talk, idle chitchat. It doesn't go anywhere and it becomes quiet again. Well, I see I am the one to break the news to them. So I tell them we have found Scott—it is the first time I have used the boy's name—and the girls show a small excitement. But of course they're confused. If we have found him, why is he not sitting here in the living room with us? They become very quiet, waiting, almost as if they are suspecting the truth. I say that somehow Scott had "fellen" into the gorge. Jesus, I think, there is no such word as "fellen." That's how upset I am—I tell the children their brother had fellen into the gorge. They ask me if he's in the hospital. I say, "Kind of." I truly do not want to be here. I try to figure some way to say it without saying he is dead. Like, He has gone away. I even think of saying he is hiding. Anything not to drop such a heavy load on them. Finally I say that he has died and gone on to a different world. They just look at me, almost as if I am their enemy. And then they start to cry; when one breaks, the other does. Their mother comes over to the couch and puts her arms around them, and I see their crushed, tear-filled faces on each side of Mother's head. I feel like I'm the guilty one, I'm the one who has caused this terrible pain.

Eventually the girls ask me questions. Where did we find him? How did it happen? And, I think, what are you going to say to them? You found him at the bottom of the gorge. One of the girls asks me if he was cold. I say no, he had his ski parka on. Again I visualize that little guy down there. The feeling I have is something like what I felt years ago with a crib death. The mother wouldn't give me the baby. I couldn't get her to let go of it. Things like that last and last with you.

The girls want to change the subject. We talk about other things. We talk about a school project with hamsters. But every few minutes it stops and gets real quiet. They're thinking. I suspect they knew their brother better than his parents did because his death seems to be not really a surprise to them. The reaction is different from what I expected. I thought they would go off the deep end. But they don't. After the initial crying they accept it. For Mom and Dad, grief has not yet had a chance to set in. But maybe they too were not entirely surprised. The night before, when we were combing the woods, I had a feeling that there was more to this thing than the father was telling us. Even if a boy is just a runaway, the parents usually know the reason, they just don't want to accept it.

The girls do what children do with a visitor in their house. They bring out their toys to show me. Very beautiful dolls, two bride dolls exactly alike. The detail work makes me a little uneasy. The doll faces are creepy, they've got a sort of sexual pout. The girls can't quite do this right; they are stuck halfway in between showing me things and being sorrowful. I can't stop seeing that yellow parka down there on the ice and knowing it was a little person. You work all your life in this job to save people, to protect them, and somehow here's one that nobody got a hold of, to snatch back from the edge.

Finally I get up. The father gets up. I approach him and put my hand on the upper part of his arm and say how sorry I am. The father's eyes say, Tell me something to make this easier. I come up empty. I go out the front door feeling that I have muffed it.

When I get back to the station house, the chief has something to show me. The officer who accompanied the boy's body to the morgue has returned with the boy's wallet, with articles of identification, and a suicide note they found in his pants pocket. The note is very simple. It says he doesn't want to live anymore. The chief mumbles, "Good-bye, cruel world." I think to myself, Shit, the boy didn't say that. I ask to see it. And it is awfully sad. It isn't dated or addressed to anybody. Just three sentences in pencil:

My reason for committing suicide is many.
My money should go wherever you want.
My time of death shall be

And his signature. Down at the bottom there are a few more lines, but they are completely crossed out so that you can't read them even when you hold it up to the light. I guess maybe he was trying to communicate with us one last time, maybe give us some explanation.

The chief says I have to go back down there and give the parents the note.

A fire bell goes off in my head. I almost yell at him. I've done my job. It's your turn now. You shoulder some of the burden. Then, once I get over thinking of myself and my own emotional stability, I consider how terrible this will be for the family. I picture the father standing there squeezing the pop can, and the mother in her pretty robe, and those two little girls. Each one of them, all four of them, will no longer be able to cling to that little shred of hope that it was accidental. No, now they'll carry the truth of the matter with them, like a stone, for the rest of their lives.

But the note is evidence. It is required by law. Suicide is a crime in this state. Which has always seemed peculiar to me—if you kill yourself, how are they going to punish you? But I can see right away that this must be entered into the record. We will have to get hold of the medical examiner so he can issue a ruling of death by suicide.

What the chief does next is extremely distasteful to me. He keeps the actual note for our records and makes a Xerox to give to the parents. A suicide note is very personal. This way, when the parents read it and hold it in their hands, it is not the actual document of their beloved son. It's gone through official channels. But the chief hands the Xerox to me and says, "The sooner it's done, the sooner it's over. No point in dragging it out and prolonging the pain."

I do not want to do it. I cannot see how I will be able to. On my way back to the fortress I make a little detour and stop at my own modest home. I go in and wash my son's breakfast dishes and sit in my living room on the edge of my black Barcalounger. I sit bent over, looking at the grain in the wood of my floor. I could use a drink. Lots of officers are heavy drinkers, as soon as they're off duty they're into the booze. Drink until the bar closes. It's sad to think that the only way you can survive is to load yourself with alcohol after working a shift. You ought to be able to have at least a few hours of enjoyment. An occasional toot is not so bad, but to have to do it day after day after day is no good at all. Look who's talking. I sit here having my drink without actually having it. I will have it, though, as soon as I'm out of uniform. Once I have got the armor off.

I toy with the idea of postponing giving them the note. I try to persuade myself that it will be easier on them. Give them twenty-four hours to get their feet under them emotionally, before they have to deal with the loss of their illusion. This note slams the door in their faces. It locks them in forever. I have almost succeeded with my little plan when I realize that it'll be in the goddamn newspaper in the morning. Not the actual note, but the only inference one can draw from it. The newspaper is no way for them to learn it. They have to be prepared. So I stand up, and I hear my voice in my living room. A sound more than a meaningful word. It startles me, my own voice. I take out the note and read it again.

> My reason for committing suicide is many.
> My money should go wherever you want.
> My time of death shall be

I study it. I notice that all three sentences begin with the word "my." And all three sentences start out like strong statements, with a definite purpose: "My reason for committing suicide is . . . ," "My money should go . . . ," "My time of death shall be. . . ." He's trying to take control over things. But each time he loses it—the reason is just "many"; his money should go "wherever you want"; the time of death is a blank. I guess the reasons really were many. I suddenly remember his friends told me that he said he had "something to do." He sure did. I know that a trained psychologist could see far more in it than I can make out. But the boy had been to trained psychologists, and what good did they do him? I wonder what he wrote at the bottom before he completely crossed it all out. That last sentence, "My time of death shall be   ." When did he think he'd fill that in? On the bridge? Come to think of it, where and when did he actually write it? In algebra class? At lunch, off by himself, so that kids wouldn't make fun of him? Maybe he wrote it at home, in his room, listening to his stereo.

Look at me. I am making it worse. You can go on with this endlessly, and see him writing it on a notebook balanced on his knee, and picture him holding the pencil as he scratches out the last lines. I'm doing what the parents will do. Trying to become him at the end. It's morbid. I can't even read it anymore because it's all blurry. Tears in my eyes. I came home for a drink, but I guess I also came home because I knew I might cry and I wanted privacy. Now my mind is all spinning, and I got to do this as well as it can be done. Actually, I wouldn't want the chief to do it even if he had offered. The chief is emotionally all thumbs. He tries, but he has this uncanny ability to say exactly the wrong thing. The parents deserve better. I can do it better. Except I don't know how to do it at all. I wish I had the real note instead of this Xerox.

I go out and stand on my porch in the bitter cold. When it gets as cold as this, it reminds you of death, the trees barren, their skeleton arms all frantic in the wind. The whole wide world itself seems utterly hopeless and forbidding. I walk down and open the door of the cruiser. I have a little fit, I can't do it, and I slink back into my house. I try to pull myself together. I walk in a big circle around my living room, three times, picking up speed. Then I am ready: I pull the front door shut behind me, get into the cruiser, and go.

It's 10:15 at night. I only got forty-five minutes left on my shift. The roads are extremely slippery—we've got a little carpet of wet snow over ice, and the salt trucks are not out yet. On my way back up a hill after a property check I manage to get the patrol car stuck in a little dip. Can't rock her out. Being a person of great pride with regard to the handling of automobiles, I don't want to call a wrecker. I call the sheriff's office. Before too long I get a response—Billy Hardesty, he's about six eight, 260, strong as a bull. He gets out of his big souped-up Dodge Diplomat, walks down, and surveys my little Ford. He opens up my trunk and climbs in, to add extra weight. We manage to get up about thirty feet from the top, where I slide onto the shoulder and get stuck again. At this point the dispatcher comes on my radio with news of a domestic in progress at the Carriage House. A neighbor called in that there was a lot of hollering going on, and now the victim herself has phoned for help. I can let it go for the eleven-to-seven man to take when he comes in, but it sounds pretty hairy. I better get there.

Hardesty senses my desire to jump into the thick of it. He says, "Open your windows." I do. He puts his huge arm around the doorpost on the passenger side. He tells

14

me to put it in gear and slowly step on the gas. I swear to God he lifts the car, with me in it, up the hill a few feet at a time. It's unbelievable. He stops and rests, and then hoists again, all the way to the top. I leave him there, doubled over, gasping for air.

The Carriage House is pretty ritzy, little town houses and a central apartment complex. My fracas is at the south end of the main building on the ground floor. The happy couple seems to have paused for a little rest between rounds when the husband finally answers my repeated loud knock. The first thing I notice is how really good-looking he is, in spite of things. I'd say he's in his midtwenties. Looks like Jesus Christ himself, long hair and a full beard and piercing dark eyes. The resemblance to our Savior ends there, however, because this fellow is drunk on his ass. And the smell of grass in the room is so thick I'll get a contact high if I take too long. The wife is tall, like her husband, and my first impression is that she is very good-looking too, underneath it all. But he has done a job on her, extensive mouth injuries, her lips all lacerated and puffed up, a big black eye beginning to develop. He must have grabbed her about the neck and hit that side of her face because her earring is embedded in her neck. I sit her down, and it takes me some time to get it loose. The earring is a little tiny pink plastic Eiffel Tower, all bloody, the hole of her pierced ear is about torn through. The most pressing problem, however, is her left hand, which he slammed in the car door. I can't tell exactly what is broken, but she can't wiggle her fingers. When I get the goddamn Eiffel Tower out of her neck, she hobbles down to the bathroom and sequesters herself in there.

Why'd they have to ruin things? It's a very tasteful apartment, books everywhere, floor to ceiling, beautiful hanging plants, modern art on the wall, and that severe kind of Danish furniture. The husband is fairly remorseful; he admits he lost control when she said things that fueled his fire. I tell him that this is no way to solve a problem. You can't do shit like this because you're angry and do not get your own way. Being pissed is no excuse to injure people. I'm giving my standard lecture, slowly and calmly. Usually when you intervene in a shouting match, they quiet right down.

But he was only resting. In spite of my telling him to leave the booze alone he stumbles back to this big vodka bottle on the sideboard in the kitchen. He gulps it down like water. I'm getting itchy, my hand on my nightstick. The wife reappears from the bathroom in a white terry-cloth robe. She's got thick brown hair that falls halfway down her back, but it's all tangled, with dried blood in it. She's smoldering, her dark eyes hot with pain and anger. She sits down with me at the dining room table and concentrates very hard on my hat, which I have laid there upside down. But her mind seems to be far away. She's in another world, not in this room. I tell her this is a very sad state of affairs. She ought to get her husband into family court; they'll issue an Order of Protection. Low in her long throat she mumbles, "Not my husband." A big bubble of bloody snot comes out of her right nostril, and it stays there until she lifts her good hand and smears it off. We sit here not saying much, except for me kind of stupidly going on about how she should have him arrested. Her mouth is so swollen it is going to be extremely difficult for her to eat for a while.

The hand should be tended to. He says he didn't mean to do that part, to the hand. He was just mad and slammed the car door to emphasize that he was. As if she didn't know that.

She stares at me with those laser dark eyes, and lets out a groan. She tries to make it back to the bathroom, but she buckles and falls on the floor. I half carry her to the bathroom, she's moaning, and she says I got to take her to the hospital. I get her seated on the toilet, but she's so wobbly I transfer her down to the floor, her back against the tub. Her eyes are really wild now. I hustle into the living room and dial for an ambulance. Holding the phone, I wait for an eternity, and then I receive notification that all the emergency vehicles are out on Route 13—a goddamn Greyhound bus went out of control on the ice and tipped over on its side. They have injured passengers. I see that I am going to have to transfer the lady. You don't want to do that for a number of reasons, one being that if they injure themselves further you are liable. And if your passenger becomes violent, you can lose control of your vehicle. But I go help her up. She's clutching her gut like it could fall out on the floor, and I get her to tell me where her coat is, and I throw that over her shoulders and wrap it around her. On the way out she crumples again, so I pick her up and carry her like my bride, wrong way across the threshold. She's a good-sized woman. As I go down the two little steps from the porch to the walk, I have happen to me what happens on nights like this to little Fords and Greyhound buses—before I know what is happening, my arms and legs go flying and I'm looking straight up at the night sky and then down I come, flat on my back, her on top of me. I black out for a second. I think I got a concussion where my head hits the ice. My breath comes back, and I roll her off me onto the snow. On my hands and knees I grab her in my arms again and struggle back to the patrol car. I stand her up, lean her against the side. Saying many intelligent things under my breath, I get her into the passenger seat, then walk around and get in behind the wheel and take off.

I go through town instead of out to the highway, which ordinarily would be faster, but we don't want to rendezvous with the Greyhound. I got to give her credit— she's biting the bullet. I'm sweating like a pig. We proceed on up to the hospital. I don't go around to the night door. I go to the big bay of emergency receiving, where the huge door is open and ambulances are unloading bus victims. The orderlies think she's another one of them, as they bounce a gurney up to our car. I don't correct them, my goal is speed. They get her up on the stretcher and wheel her into the emergency room. I back the patrol car out of the way—I can hear more sirens behind us, coming up the hill.

I linger. For some reason I cannot go off duty. I can't leave the hospital. It gets to be one-thirty, two-thirty, and I tell myself that I am not leaving until she is upstairs safe in a room. The staff is like on "M*A*S*H" with incoming wounded, the whole area jumping. I am sympathetic to the suffering of all the Greyhound passengers, but I do not want my girl to get lost in the shuffle. I still have not quite recovered my senses from cracking my head on the ice. I get a nurse and I become a little panicky when we check all the stalls in ER and can't find our patient. The nurse sends me out to the waiting room while she tries to sort out what is happening. I have just finished my cigarette under a Thank You For Not Smoking sign when the nurse returns with news that our girl's in the OR right now. I say I am going to stay until she is out of danger. I lose consciousness and do not regain it until the nurse is shaking me by the shoulder. She wants information that I do not have. I promise I'll provide it as soon as I can get back to work. As for now, the patient has been transferred upstairs. I am able to find her room and tiptoe in and sit with her in the dim light. They've cleaned her up pretty good, she's sleeping, her hand in a cast, an IV in her other arm. I sit in an extremely comfortable chair, and I guess I doze off again, because I don't get out of there until almost four.

I zip up the hill back to the station, only to realize I left my hat at the Carriage House. The chief is a fiend on the matter of our hats. So I swing by the Carriage House to retrieve it. When I pull up to the building, I see Mr. Jesus Hippie Asshole outside, down by the garbage cans. "Hi!" he says, like I'm his friend. And I just go crazy, I pounce on the bastard. I don't even know I am doing it. I slam him up against the brick, garbage cans clattering and rolling away. I grab him by the collar with both hands—I about shake his teeth out. I chuck the back of his head into the brick. I yell, "How do you like it? How do you like it?" Then I throw him headlong across the snowy gravel. I get him inside and his hands are all cut up and the knees of his pants are torn. I dump him semiconscious on the couch and realize what I have done and what kind of trouble I am probably in for. The punk will file charges of police brutality, and what can I say? He wasn't resisting arrest. I just lost it.

I get a whole roll of paper towels from the kitchen and clean him up a bit. I roll him on his side. He's bleeding from the back of the head. Not too bad. He'll live. I say if she decides to prosecute, I will leave no stone unturned until I find him. He seems to get the point.

I don't really come to my senses until I'm back at the station, out of uniform and standing under a hot shower. Everything's been going a mile a minute in my head, and now I am able to slow it down. I force myself to sit in my civilian clothes at the desk and make out a preliminary report. It's almost six o'clock when I arrive home, totally exhausted. If I don't have myself a drink, I'm going to explode. But first I stop in my little kitchen and make Dick's breakfast, the way I always do, the grapefruit sections, the bread in the toaster, the cereal in the bowl. It takes but a few moments, just my way of saying good morning. Or to be honest about it, I can't say good morning to him in person because of the next thing I do. I crack a tray of ice cubes into a bowl and carry it down the hall past two bedrooms to my den. There, in my womblike retreat, I crouch down and reach into my closet. I go way in the back behind everything and grab a pint of Cutty Sark from the half-empty case. From the bottom drawer of my big knotty-pine desk I extract my long-stemmed glass.

Most people don't realize policemen have their own problems. The front you put on is cold and calculated, as if you could handle the world's problems without becoming involved. You put on a stiff exterior. You try to be gentle, of course. And you try to be kind. You try to work things out so that people feel better. But it takes a toll on you. It takes a little piece away from you that you may not have wanted to be taken.

Your own personal life gets interrupted constantly. Your shifts are never guaranteed. You have no time for yourself. In a complicated case you have tons of things to do and you frequently run out of hours. You can't stop a case in midstream, go home and sleep, and take your day off. Things have to be seen through to conclusion. After many, many years you become calloused, and you do not react to things that occur in your jurisdiction as you did when you were a rookie. You build compartments in the back of your head, automatic responses, instructions on how you should act. But occasionally you do get involved, you become friends with people. Most times you don't see them again; it's the last complaint you'll ever get from them. A very urgent matter to them, paramount in their minds, is for you just another in a long series of pestering complaints. But you handle it for them, you pretend it's vitally important. They pay their taxes to pay you. But it takes a toll on your feelings and affects how you are at home. Sometimes you just have to go off by yourself and get away from everybody.

Most policemen work two jobs. Most policemen I know have been divorced at least once. That's the price you pay when you become an officer. Rookies don't know that. Some do not last long; they work a year or two and then find something where they get the weekend off. Your wife has the weekend off, and you get tired of missing picnics.

A policeman is two different people. A split personality. When you're off duty and home, you're one type of person. When you're working, you put on a suit of armor. Nothing leaks in and nothing leaks out. Every day you check to make sure all the leaks are stopped up. If you didn't, your emotions would drive you crazy. So you put on your uniform, put on your armor. It's a false front. Cold and unemotional, everything under control, don't take anything in, other than what you have to write down in notes for reports. Don't let any of your emotions out.

Although, like tonight, sometimes you fail. What I did to that guy bothers me. I only went crazy like that once before, ten or twelve years ago, a child abuser. It was back when we worked partners, and the chief and I were riding around checking things here and there. About noon we received a call from a woman who said she saw a man take a girl into the bushes, and she could hear her crying. We immediately responded, down to the playground at the lake. It was between the pavilion and the rest rooms. A big hedge. It was an extremely hot day, in the nineties, and the chief and I were hyped up a bit. You always think the worst. I mean, looking back on it, what if the man had been the girl's father and was just changing her panties? The area was pretty isolated, all the people were down by the ball fields. The chief suddenly shouted, "Stop," and we could see him. He had one arm around the back of her shoulder, holding her dress up, and her panties were down around her ankles. He was about to put his hand between her legs. Whether he'd already done it before, I of course wouldn't know. All I could see was this guy in the bushes and her little bare butt. She seemed to be about nine or ten, the age of Kitty, the daughter of the woman I was living with at the time.

Which probably is what made me go crazy. We ran over to the hedge, and I grabbed him and dragged him out of there and ran him straight into the side of the patrol car. The chief took care of the little girl, who was hysterical, crying, though I don't think he had done anything to her—you couldn't see any damage. Once the chief got the girl quieted down, he joined me, and we really put it to the bastard. We popped him six ways to Sunday. I finally cuffed him, as tight as I could, just to hurt him. We located the girl's mother, who took her up to the hospital, and they found no damage. He hadn't touched her. Or just touched her. We ran him up to the hospital, too. I hoped they'd cut his throat. Both the chief and I had been out of control, which is not customary; one man usually stays calm—good cop, bad cop.

When we brought the guy back to the station for booking, there was this giant lesbian sitting there on the bench in handcuffs, a bad check charge had turned into a physical fracas. So she's sitting there, and the chief and I are dealing with this idiot. We charge him with resisting arrest, sexual abuse, and endangering the welfare of a minor. This lesbian is fairly good size, the man in the relationship—she's very mannish—and has been in a lot of scraps. She looks over at us and says, "Take these cuffs off me for a minute."

"What for?" we ask.

She says, "I'll fix that dirty son of a bitch so he won't bother any more little girls."

We thought about it. We looked at each other. We were tempted. The guy was getting really nervous. But the chief and I had regained our composure, we had our armor back on. Besides, you couldn't do it in the station house at midday. Maybe we could have got away with it in the parking lot at night.

You can say the abusive guy has it coming to him. You can debate until the cows come home whether it is ever justified to solve such problems violently. But if you do choose violence, you should go home and change your clothes first. Soil your hands, not the uniform. You must do everything the way you are supposed to. Everything has its own purpose and reason. There is a certain point which you do not go beyond, or you'll find yourself drained. If you don't do things the correct way, you won't last more than a year. The public takes this as your being unfeeling. They don't realize that you handle hundreds of these cases a year, and if you give of yourself every time and become emotionally involved, you can't function. You just get bogged down in feelings and let your heart run away with you. You don't help anybody. A policeman is a miniature psychologist running around patching things that have taken years to develop. You carry this little bag of patches with you, like for fixing inner tube leaks, and every time something pops up, you throw a patch on it, and then you get another call and you go throw a patch on that, and you spend your entire career patching things—you don't really fix anything. Patch them up and get them to somebody who can take care of the problem.

What was it I said to Mr. Jesus Asshole as I was making his teeth rattle? "How do you like it?" I think that's what I said. I run back and forth between satisfaction and guilt. On the one hand, I cleaned that sucker's clock. On the other, I stained the armor.

When you get home after duty, it's like you throw a

switch; you turn from one kind of creature into another kind of creature. Mr. Armor is suddenly Mr. Human. Some policemen can make that transition. Others cannot. Those that cannot have problems. They become drinkers, like me. They become ex-husbands, like me. Unlike me, some become very cynical and hard-hearted. Lose their compassion for people. They have a very sad life. They can't dispel the pressures of the job. Can't live a normal life, or seminormal, enjoy the finer things, read a good book, go to a show, deal pleasantly with the wife and kids.

Most policemen have very few friends. Friends are the people you can tell your real feelings to. Without any friends you gradually get to feel angry inside. Frustrated. No close friends you can sit down with. So you keep it all locked up inside. In all the years I have been a policeman, I don't know anybody I've ever actually sat down with and told my true feelings to. Maybe the actual public doesn't have a friend, either. I wouldn't know. But I think they surely must have somebody they can talk to. A policeman trusts nobody. All those feelings under lock and key. I don't know if a normal person would have that type of friendship, but I should think there would always be somebody who is at least a possibility. You'd only need one. But how do you know that this person you tell your inner feelings to won't take them and use them against you? Or scoff at you? Even wives and girlfriends. So you never actually unload. I think it's because a policeman sees so much bullshit in his life that he loses his faith in humanity. Also, in addition to the fear of getting spurned, there is the very strong chance that if you let it all out, then you would have to deal with it.

I always try to treat people fairly and with compassion. I'm a problem solver. Sometimes I'll spend a whole Sunday just stopping and shooting the shit with people who are mowing their lawns. There's a whole number of old people I watch. I check their houses to see if they're in trouble, or have gone away, or if they're dead. I've found several dead senior citizens. I go out of my way to be part of the community. Too many officers just come in, work their eight hours, and go home. But I am always doing a whole array of diddly-shit that nobody requires me to. I try to be polite. I can be an asshole too, and if they use bad language, I use bad language. But if they're polite, I'm polite.

When you come home after a shift, you have had eight hours of problems. You don't want any more. After a while you walk around with your eyes crossed. You look for the negative in everything. That is why having a policeman for a father is difficult. Kids hate cops. I know I did. You would not like to be the child of a policeman. The parent who is an officer is too strait-laced, too strict. In your work as a policeman, you see so much bullshit that you tend to lecture a lot. You try to steer your children away from trouble, and what you do is drive them right into it. Your own kids become wild and uncontrollable. Dad's shifts, his constant absence from home, problems with the mother, problems which get to be so extreme that often there is no mother. All the lectures, you tend to browbeat and cajole.

Maybe that's what's wrong between me and my son. Dick and I used to get along fine. But now we seem to be at each other's throats most of the time. The biggest sore spot for me is that he doesn't want to go to college. If I had to pinpoint the number-one regret of my life, it would be that I didn't go to college. I know I would have enjoyed it. And it's a ticket to all the higher things. There is so much interesting shit I know nothing about. With college-educated people I can't hold up my end of the conversation. Not that I am stupid. I'm just ignorant. My whole life would be different, and far better, if I had gone to college. Dick could handle the work; down at the high school he gets all A's and B's without half trying. And it's not like he has anything else in mind. He has no career objectives at all. Can't seem to look beyond the end of his nose. Seventeen years old, bright as a dime, he is already taking a backseat in life. He's a big rangy kid, rawboned, almost as tall as me now and still shooting up. His gray eyes just shout at you how smart he is.

And our problems may have nothing to do with my being a policeman. I pride myself on keeping my drinking private. Not to let it spill over into his life. But there have been times when I have trapped myself—the game plan changed, and I was too looped to adjust. Just the other night Dick told me he was going to bring his new girl-friend, Rebecca, back to the house after the movie, around 11:00 P.M. When I got off a particularly distressful shift at 3:00, I had the house to myself. I got out the old Cutty and I was sitting in the dining room, pretty stupid, feeling sorry for myself. I was planning to tie it on good and then just be asleep in my own room so that they could have the run of the place. Then, suddenly, at 6:30, here they are. He's come back to dress up for dinner and she's right with him. Rebecca's a top student, I hear, plays the flute in the orchestra. I made every effort to straighten up and fly right. But there are limits to what you can do. The two of them stood there in the hallway, her eyes kind of alarmed, his eyes averted. The awkwardness of it. You want to introduce your girl to your father proudly. And instead you're ashamed. Dad's a drinker, it's a family problem. I talked too much, trying to cover, digging my hole deeper. I called Dick back into my den and whispered, "Jesus, man, you said *after* the movie." The anger and disappointment in those gray eyes. I wanted to disappear. But they were the ones who disappeared. I got myself sober—I napped and then drank a whole pot of coffee. But Dick didn't bring her back. He'd learned his lesson.

Can't say I've learned mine. I open the bottle. I pour. The first one is without ice, neat. I sit and stare at the golden liquid in the long-stemmed glass. And then I sip formally, as if I am dining out. It kicks in, all through my body, flooding me with warmth. There. That's the ticket.

Sunday evening I am drenched in gloom and the sports section, sitting in my black Barcalounger. Dick said dinner at six, and now it's eight. Where is that boy? I have turned off the heat under the bag of broccoli in cream sauce. The Caesar salad I was so proud of is wilting in the fridge. Then I notice this funny light reflected on the ceiling, an amber rotary light coming from outside. I hop to my front window and there's a Triple A tow truck out there on the street with its moonball going. My heart starts to pound because the truck has got Dick's little blue Chevy hung up there behind him like a dead junker. I tear out of my house in my slippers. Dick pops out of the truck and meets me in the middle of the front lawn. His eyes are all funny, and I frantically check him for concussion, whiplash. But he seems to be okay, just slow. Beer on his breath. He says, "Dad, the windshield got a crack in it." I'm still checking him out for damage, but I see that he has been drinking and smoking pot on Sunday night, a school night. I trudge in my slippers to investigate the damage to the Chevy.

You say the windshield's got a crack in it? Looks more like somebody threw a baseball through it. There's a hole in the windshield about the size of a grapefruit. And the front bumper's all mashed in, the fender crum-

pled. A Puerto Rican kid with a moustache is at the
wheel of the tow truck, and I tell him to take it down to
Cowan's Chevytown on Route 13. We'll follow in my car.
Dick and I get into my rusty Olds, and I ask him what
the hell happened. He mumbles that he was just listening
to music and then decided to take a spin. There was no
other car involved. Dick sits beside me like laundry. He
says he called the Triple A from a farm house.

A farm house?

Down at Chevytown I sign the Triple A forms and
give the Puerto Rican kid a ten spot. Dick and I go home
to a ruined dinner. In the morning I tell the Chevytown
service manager that I was driving. My little way of
teaching the lad a lesson in personal responsibility. And
Dick's just pissed that he can't have his car for a week.
That seems to be the only emotion he feels.

A week goes by. Finally the parts come in, and the
Chevy is good as new. I do not let him drive it by himself;
I have to ride with him. He thinks this is cruel and
unusual punishment. But I see he doesn't know his
vehicle at all. Does not brake for cats and dogs. Every
second we are in the car, I am finding fault with him, and
all we do is yell at each other. One evening when I am
imposing the humiliation of riding with him, I notice
that at every corner he has to stop and look hither and
yon. I ask him why, and I discover that my son can't read
the street signs; he has to stop and squint. Lo and behold,
my son needs glasses. I thought there was some funny
business at the DMV when he didn't take the eye test
and instead had a note from an oculist. It turns out that
Dick thinks he'd look wimpy in glasses, which is why
he sits in the front row of all his classes, so he can read

what's on the board. He has been driving a car all this time without being able to *see* the goddamn cats and dogs. So we buy him some John Lennon granny glasses, and they don't make him look wimpy at all. He's shocked to see all the shit in the world, like the leaves on the trees. Myself, I had watched him draw the footstool right up close to the TV screen, and never realized he was nearsighted.

The passion of his life is soccer. The coach says Dick plays more intelligently than the other guys, who just throw themselves all over the field with a lot of wasted energy. It's like his eyes are in the back of his head, or like he's not watching the game at ground level, because he's always where the ball is, sometimes before it gets there. All during the fall season, even when I was on a three-to-eleven shift, I'd find some excuse to get down to the goose pasture and watch the game. Stand out there in the rain. Then one day the coach stopped and told me how surprised and disappointed he was to see Dick's name on that statement. "Statement?" I said, "what statement?" Eventually I found out that Dick's best friend, Erik, was quitting the team, and Dick was going to quit with him. I knew why Erik wanted to quit. In the Oswego game, Erik was on defense, guiding the ball back to our goalie. Erik dug his left foot into the turf and swung his right foot at the ball, and he must have caught his toe in the mud because he lost his concentration and kicked the ball in this big arc, and it sailed over our own goalie's head and into the net. Erik had scored a goal for the other team. Nobody could quite believe it, least of all Erik. He just stood there, and then, real slowly, he just fell backward like a board, flat on his back. I thought to myself, Shit, the kid will remember this all his life. And he probably will. He couldn't seem to recover himself. Didn't go to school that Monday, or Tuesday, either. He didn't come over to our house like he always used to. Dick didn't come home afternoons because he was over at Erik's. Dick told me that the guys gave Erik a nickname, "Score." They'd make little jokes about Erik "scoring," like with a girl. Erik couldn't take it. So he decided to quit. He wrote that "statement" and got Dick to sign it, too.

But how could Dick quit what he loved so much and was so good at? Once I saw him come up out of nowhere and save a goal. Five of the enemy team were bearing down to score, and then all at once Dick was just there, in this blur of jerseys and legs, and he saved the day with a header that about broke my own teeth just watching it. When the horn sounded and it was over, the guys came around and slapped his back. I, of course, was bursting my buttons. At such moments you realize how much you have invested in your child. It's kind of horrible. Nauseating, actually.

I told him not to quit the team. It was a bad break for Erik, but quitting is no way to deal with adversity. If Erik's going to drown, there's no point in drowning with him. Then I caught myself and stepped back. I said to myself, Well, Dick's got to make his own choices in this life. Let him make his mistakes and learn from them. But I knew I was right. Besides which, I'd never been too sure about Erik anyway. The boy can't look you in the eye. No wonder the other guys on the team go after him. And now they were going after Dick, too, because he rides on the team bus with Erik, and the guys called them the Bobbsey twins. I said, "Don't let Erik drag you down with him." I knew right away that was a mistake—I do not want to teach my son to turn his back on a friend in trouble. I could see that if Erik was all alone by himself, then that was all the more reason for Dick to stand by him. But now the two of them didn't shower with the team; they went home and showered at Erik's house. I didn't like that showering at all. I visualized the Bobbsey twins playing Drop the Soap. And, to give him credit, Dick didn't quit the team. We made it to Sectionals. Dick got an assist on a goal; he drilled it across the field to Richie, who caught the high right corner of the net. On the following Monday afternoon I heard my son in the confines of his bedroom. He had pulled the phone in there, and he was whispering, probably to Rebecca, "You see my name in the newspaper?" He was plenty proud. If he had quit the team, he would not have had that experience.

And at the awards banquet he got this big gold plaque, the Scholar-Athlete Award. Imagine, this scholar-athlete won't go to college. I can't understand it. After the awards were all given out, the coach put his arm around both Dick and me and said, laughing, "I could have *strangled* this guy for trying to quit the team." I was beaming away—and Dick shot me a look that almost decked me right there in the cafeteria. On the way home I asked him about it, and he would hardly talk to me. He went over to Erik's house and came home stoned—*stoned*, the son of a police officer! To my great relief we hadn't had any arguments about dope, because he had been in training and did not want any controlled substance messing up his body. But now there was a little burned brown hole in his green varsity letter. He stomped into his room and slammed the door. Eventually he came out, with a towel around him, and in his dope fog he bumped into me on his way to a midnight shower, with that long cleat mark on his bulgy left calf where he got spiked and played bleeding through his sock. He growled, "Just let's not talk about *college!*" I went into his room and took the plaque out of his waste basket—I don't think he really would have thrown it away. I sat on his bed, the plaque on my lap, and listened to the water run. You'd think it would be a night to remember, when your son wins the Scholar-Athlete Award. But Dick and I have fallen way down to the bottom of a deep dark hole. We can't seem to climb out.

In the dead of night, Saturday, the phone rings. I stumble up out of sleep, and it's him. He says, "Dad, you remember that agreement we signed?" It takes me a minute and then I remember: if he's at a party and he's been overcelebrating, he is not to try to drive home. He is to call me to come pick him up. My sleep-befuddled brain takes note, with pleasure, that he's living up to the bargain. He's not sure quite where he is, at 3:00 A.M., but it's a party at somebody's house. His voice is real hushy, so the party won't hear, although I hear no party in the background. He says, "How about that Mobil station next to Highway Hi-Fi? On Route 13?"

"No problem," I say. "Be there in ten minutes."

"Thanks, Dad," he says in a funny, grown-up whisper, like we are plotting a conspiracy, and hangs up.

I stand here naked in the chilly hall. I try to clear my head.

I climb into my clothes and hobble to the front closet. I put on my raunchy old coat. I go out into the frozen night and get into my Olds with its personalized license plate, 1 GROUCH. I back out the driveway. I go ka-whangy all over the snowy road in the darkness. I'm tooling along here all drowsy and cold, can't seem to wake up. I whip over to Route 13, and when I arrive at the Mobil station, I snap wide awake. A county sheriff's car is pulled up behind Dick's blue Chevy. An officer has got Dick standing out there in the headlights. What's he doing, running a breathalyzer on him? I coast in beside the neon red and white Coke machine. I jump out of my Olds and I say, "I'm his father." I really bark it. Dumb, very dumb. But Dick's eyes go, *Thanks*, because he is having no fun at all. The officer is a rookie, I've not met him or even seen him before. He says to me, kind of nervous and angry, "This permit means he can go to school and straight home. No side trips to party." He's gruff as can be, and his hat's too big for him—it sits loose on his razor cut. I'm thinking, Don't run a number on my kid—you're just a kid yourself. He shines his flashlight in my face. I put my hand up, and I think of tinning him, but I decide to wait on that. Let's see if Dick can get out of this little difficulty on his own. It's so cold out here. I wonder if the officer has a pretty little bride at home keeping his bed all snug and warm for him. He sees the impatience in my eyes, and he is just a kid, and I do not want to make a blustery fool of myself in front of my son. He relaxes and says, "I didn't know if we had a burglary in progress or what."

Dick's looking at him very seriously.

The rookie says to me, "Your son's a class six, he's driving out of class." I am smiling in my head, running through the various classes in my head. The rookie goes on in the dead of night, a stickler for detail. "He drove his vehicle from the party to here, and that's out of class." He can't seem to get beyond it.

I remember doing that when I was his age, dorking a person with a detail like that, when in my head I was really trying to figure out what I was going to do next, whether to issue a citation or wave the guppy on. I think a shit-eating grin is beginning to play around the corners of my mouth. Finally I say, "Why are we standin' out here freezin' our nuts off? The boy called me. Don't rag on him for doin' the right thing."

The cop considers this point and dispatches it into his back brain for data evaluation. Shit, he is young. Dick and he could change clothes, and the world would not be the wiser. Finally our constable on patrol blinks and says to Dick, "Well, let this be a warning to you. You're lucky I didn't catch you on the street. I'd have to write you up."

A dispatcher's voice blasts something on the radio in the sheriff's car, and the young officer looks at us with a little scowl. He gets back into his vehicle and slams the door on himself, backs out of the station, and guns her up 13.

I say to Dick, "Want to follow me home?"

"I'm really not feelin' so hot, Dad."

"Drink too much at the party?"

"Yeah, a *quart* of Cream Ale. I drank it really fast."

"Dumb."

"I know. At the beginning it was fun, everybody was

there. But at the end there were only five people. Totally
trashed. And no music. It was so quiet. It was like
despair."

"I've been to parties like that. Sometimes I've had
them just for myself."

He smiles at me sheepishly. "I really folded." And
then he stops, like he's listening to something way far
away. His head goes up like a deer. And then he loses it—
Dick tosses his cookies right into the snow. I pat him on
his back as he bends over. I can't believe I find it a little
funny, me of all people, but many is the time ol' Dad has
done this, wrapped around the china lover. I pat him
some more, and he straightens up and sighs, and sighs
again.

I say, "You'll feel better now."

His severely bloodshot eyes are wide and frightened.
We walk it off. He's catching his breath. He mutters,
"God what a shitty party." Eventually, retracing our steps
in the snow, he says, "I really don't feel like driving."

"Okay," I say. "Let's leave your Chevy here. Pick it
up in the morning." But we can't leave it here by the
pump. So I get in and crank it into reverse, and back it
out and park it way over off the apron between two rusted
junkers. I lock it, and think I might leave a note on the
windshield, but I don't have paper and pen. Dick's already
got himself ensconced in the suicide seat of 1 GROUCH.
I climb in behind the wheel and take off back up 13.

I say, "How ya doin'?"

He says, "I think I feel better."

We get off 13 at Lake and go the quick way up Wren
to Klein, hang a right on Maplewood, and pull into our
own driveway. We drag ourselves into the house.

Dick stands in the dining room. He yawns. Finally he blunders by me and makes his way into the bathroom. I watch him stand there at the toilet, hands on his hips, taking a long leak of Cream Ale. Then he goes and stands in his room, slowly rocking toe-heel-toe. Slowly he sheds his clothes. I'm so tired that I match him article for article, until we are both standing here in our underpants, stupidly staring at each other. I say, "Wash your face." He looks at me so sad that I go into the bathroom and soak a washcloth and wring it out a little, bring it back into his room, and he scrubs around uselessly, with no heart in it. Cold water dribbles down onto his chest. He stands there like the Leaning Tower of Pisa. I think he'll be asleep before his head hits the pillow. But as he flops down on his big double bed, his eyes are open; he's sober. He says, "You know what's shitty?"

"What?"

"When you're a little kid you don't notice. But then you get older. And you begin to wonder if anybody's really happy. You thought they were, but then you see they were just covering up."

I nod. I say, "I was proud of you tonight."

"You were?"

"For calling me to come pick you up—"

"I cannot believe what a klutz I was, showing him my permit. He was talking so fake, like it wasn't really him. Like you wouldn't know if he had any hobbies."

"He's young." I wait. I say, "I mean I'm proud you lived up to your end of our agreement." I stick my thumb up. "Good job."

Dick looks at me. He says, "You don't know how much that means to me."

I motion for him to slide over, and he does, and I crawl into his bed beside him. We lie here. Damn, his mattress is better than mine.

He says, "Have you noticed how people have magic words?"

"Magic words?"

"A magic word for a person is a word they can visualize emotionally."

My, my, listen to the boy—visualize emotionally. "What's my magic word?"

Dick's asleep. I think he's asleep. But not quite. He mumbles his father's magic word: "Job."

I think. I guess it's true. My job is who I am. A policeman. My job is To Protect and Serve. For my policeman job I've got the armor. But I've got no armor where you are concerned. I say, "You know one thing I really regret?"

"Not going to college."

"Yes. But I mean when you came into the house with Becky, and I had been drinking. There I stood, sloshed in front of your girlfriend."

He says, half in dreamland, "I regret it too."

"I imagine."

Another silence, and then he says, "No, I mean I regret what I felt. I was glad."

"Glad?"

He wakes up a little. "I remember thinking—*Good!* I was glad you were drunk. I didn't want you to be on top of things and make her think you were a cool father, even if you are a cop. I didn't want her to say to me, 'Gee, your dad's a neat guy.' I wanted her to feel *sorry* for me."

And now, just when he should be falling asleep, he's

crying. He says, all hot and flustered, "And that means I wanted my dad to be sick!"

I reach into the box of Kleenex on his night stand. I hand him one. He wipes his eyes and blows his nose. He sighs. He's seventeen, and he's a little boy. Like the little boy he used to be. But now he's big, those sweat glands working away so that he almost smells like a man. His head falls bonk against my shoulder. He gulps, and sighs again, and then he does finally fall asleep. I stay perfectly still.

Her name is weird for a female. Sydney. It seems to me like a name for a blond wimpy guy. Not her at all. But that's who she is. When I go up to the hospital to see how she's doing, I discover why she won't press charges against Mr. Jesus Asshole. It takes a while to come out, and I don't want to tire her; she's still in a good bit of pain. The worst part is not the broken hand. It's her mouth, they had to put stitches in her lips. In my mind I am thinking what I always think when I deal with victims of rape or bad physical abuse. After a while I say it out loud to her: "You know, if you don't put out a complaint against this guy, he is free to go do it to somebody else."

She is embarrassed. Her eyes dart away and go all around the room. Then she looks at me, and says, "He's my student." She says, real low and clearly ashamed, "A big mistake." Pause. She looks away again.

We stay away from the subject after that. She clearly does not want to discuss it further. She is actually pretty self-possessed for a person who has been through such an ordeal.

I don't go visit her in the hospital again. I don't want her to think I'm pushy or overbearing. But I'm worried about her. After a couple of days go by, I am investigating a noise complaint at the Carriage House one evening, and I see the lights on in her apartment. So I stop in. I am cheered up to find her considerably improved. She hasn't gone back to teaching her classes yet, but she's alert and in fairly good spirits. She makes me a cup of coffee, and I put my hat upside down on the table where I put it the first time. Of course I do not tell her anything about what I did to the guy later that night. I say, "It must be kind of hard for you to do grocery shopping with that cast on your hand. Give me a list, and I'll be glad to pick up a few things."

She says, "Oh, thank you, don't bother, I can manage."

I say, "I frequently do it for sick people, old people."

Then, with this wan little smile on her poor lips, she says, "Well, you know, maybe you could."

So I do.

After a week we got a little friendship started. I stop in after work, just to chat, and when we get a big snowfall, I shovel her walk. She's pretty isolated; I guess she doesn't want people to see the damage. She'd have to explain. I love her outfits. She dresses unlike any woman I have known. Maybe it's the name Sydney. She wears mannish clothes, men's shirts and sport coats and even a pair of brown wing-tip shoes just like a pair of Florsheims I once had. It tickles me, her cowboy boots and big hat. Although, she does seem quite feminine. She wears bright stockings and has a whole array of big pins. Always got one on like a badge, big gold and silver pins of airplanes and horses and a cat-and-a-fiddle and a big silver star with Star Taxi on it.

I can't figure her out. But I like her a whole bunch.

She's a big breezy woman. She smokes too much, like me, and we sit at that table lighting up one right after another. We are on totally different planes intellectually. She's finishing her thesis for her doctorate. But she doesn't make me feel like a clod. A couple of my remarks on the opposite sex make her eyebrows go up. I think, though, it's mainly the twenty years difference in our ages, I haven't mastered the new ways of thinking. Her brown eyes are real smart. Warm. We laugh a lot. That is, she laughs, and I wonder what it was I just said. But she's more amused than scornful, and I don't feel cast out. We take potshots at each other; she makes fun of my views, and I make fun of her clothes.

One day when I get off work at three, I stop by and she is in a dither. "I'm going back to work!" she proudly announces. But she's not at full strength yet, and she's worried about how she'll do.

I say I'll be glad to drive her over to the college and pick her up after. She hesitates. I say, "I got nothing to do. I'm off work, and my son's in this indoor soccer league. The guys always go to McDonald's afterward, so I don't have to fix his dinner."

"Well," she says, "come to my class."

"Come to your class?"

"It's a big course, you'll be lost in the shuffle. I'm showing them a movie in the auditorium."

"What's the movie?"

"On the Waterfront."

I say, "I think I saw that when it first came out." I actually don't remember it so hot. I must've been only about fourteen.

She's rushing about in her baggy pants, leaving ciga-

rette butts here and there in ashtrays, starting for the
door and then remembering her briefcase. Finally I say,
"Calm down. You'll drive us both nuts. I'll come to the
movie."

We take her car, which is a piece of shit, a tinny old
Honda Accord. The engine's so far out of tune it's not
even funny; it coughs and sputters and dies at stop signs.
We finally pull into a space right next to the auditorium
and walk in, the two of us dressed like men. I hang back
so no eyebrows will be raised. I sit in the very last row,
the way I did in all my classes in high school. I even
pretend I am in high school again—I turn up the collar of
my coat like Elvis. By 4:00 P.M. there are forty or fifty
kids in the place, and Sydney down in front makes an
announcement or two, very professional. It tickles me
the way she tries to hide her hand in the cast, which only
draws attention to it. Then the lights in the auditorium
go down and the movie comes on.

Gradually it comes back to me. Especially when
Marlon Brando tells the priest to go to hell. I remember
how that startled the piss out of me, at fourteen. And
that scene in the backseat of the car, Marlon Brando
talking with his brother: Charlie, Charlie, you should
have taken care of me. I sit like in high school, pretending
to be bored and not paying attention.

When it's over the lights come back up, and they
have a little discussion period. Sydney really knows her
stuff. She has a lot of background on the McCarthy
period, when the movie was made, and the problem of
"naming names." Some of the guys who made the movie
and acted in it were members of the Communist party.
They had to face the very same problem as Terry Malloy,

to testify against their buddies. What I like the most is what she says about the ending. She says the movie was based on some articles about corruption in the dockworker unions. Articles in newspapers or magazines or whatever. And the real-life situation ended in defeat. The Terry Malloy character in real life did not nail the racketeers. Sydney says, "Imagine the movie ending that way." She says the Hollywood tradition always shows the triumph of good over evil, and everything comes out all right in the end. Hollywood heroes have to win. Like here, they get the girl. "But," Sydney says, "Brando is much more interesting when he's a loser than when he changes into a hero. Think what it would be like to have him see the light, and then not be able to change anything. In Hollywood, once you see the right thing to do, you are able to do it. But life doesn't work that way. The movie asks a deep question, and then gives a shallow answer."

I'm sitting here in the back row with my feet up on the chair in front of me. I am thinking that she is correct. My line of work has certainly impressed me with that. And I'm thinking what a bright lady Sydney is. She's forgotten about her cast, and she's gesturing a lot. Kids crowd around her afterward. I wait out in the hall, walking up and down, smoking.

On the way home in her pathetic Honda, she's all exhilarated. She was afraid of it, and now she's relieved to have it behind her. I tell her I think she was excellent. We go into her apartment. She has a brandy, in a big snifter, to celebrate her Return to the Classroom. I shouldn't, but I make myself a neat little sidecar. I sip real slow. I know how it can run away with me if I'm not careful. She just gulps hers down and gets a little flushed in the face. She loves her job. She says, *"On the Waterfront* just knocks me out. The sexiest moment I've ever seen on the screen is when Brando and Eva Marie Saint are talking in the playground. Remember that scene?"

I nod.

She says, "He sits there in the swing and plays with her glove. Absently puts it on and works his fingers into it." She looks at me, and she says, "What's the sexiest moment you ever saw?"

Right away I think Marilyn Monroe. There's this scene in *Some Like It Hot* that I always watch on "The Late Show" whenever it's on. She's in the rest room of the train going to Florida, and she's banging away with an ice pick at a big block of ice, to make cubes for drinks, and she tells Tony Curtis about all the clarinet players who have taken advantage of her and left her holding the bag. She just rattles on, whacking away at that big block of ice, hardly realizing what she's saying. She's so gorgeous and so vulnerable, your dick goes up and your heart goes out. I don't put it that way to Sydney, but whatever it is I manage to get into words seems to please her. We send out for a pizza, and I don't get out of there until almost eleven. We stand at her door for a minute or two, can't quite let go.

In 1 GROUCH on the way home I kick up my heels. It's what I always imagined college would be like, to catch a flick and go out for coffee afterward and talk it over. I want Dick not to miss out on it. I mean, just to look at a movie that way, instead of letting it wash over you all passively. In my job the truth of the matter is frequently painful, and nothing can be done about it. You don't pursue the truth, you bury truth, and move on. And even the truth is bullshit. I have often thought about the professional help we get for people. You say a guy needs counseling, he's got psychological problems. That's not the truth. You can give a person all the personality profiles you want, but it's not a psychological problem. Sometimes what is wrong with him is that he's poor. Once you straighten him out psychologically he's worse off than before. Like what Sydney said about Terry Malloy. You take a person's personality disorder away, and then he can see just how deep the shit is that he's standing in.

I think about the last time I was with a woman where I really put everything into it. Patsy. Patsy Pullman, Realtor. She sold me my house. Patsy and I lived together for two years. I was crazy about her. We would have got married if it hadn't been for her daughter. Which sounds terrible. It is. It wasn't Kitty's fault. She couldn't help what was wrong with her. I still don't know what it was, though I have my suspicions, as I did at the time. I didn't know how to say it to Patsy. We'd talk for hours and hours.

Patsy's ex-husband, Kitty's father, moved to Ohio and had custody of Kitty that year. I guess I could have seen the whole sorry business when he mailed us her report card. Kitty was smart as a whip, way ahead of her grade. The teacher said that when she was out of the room, she'd have Kitty read to the class. But there was this long handwritten note stapled to the report card. The teacher said Kitty had some severe emotional problems which seemed to center on sex. You didn't let her go to the bathroom with another child, or you'd find them both in there with their pants down. She cried a lot, right out of the blue for no apparent reason. And she always had to bring an extra set of clothes to school because she'd wet her pants. I read in Ann Landers ten warning signals of child abuse. Kitty had seven. Like reverting to infantile behavior, wetting their beds, sucking their thumbs. They cram things in their mouths, shoelaces and crayons. Kitty was always sucking on this little mashed-up hanky. They're too eager to please and always giving you things—like Kitty took her teacher one of her daddy's girlfriend's necklaces. And they are without "affect," not so much sad as no expression at all. Which was the way Kitty would get. But the big problem was getting her mother, Patsy, to admit that anything was wrong. Even with that long note stapled to the report card, Patsy only saw Kitty's success in reading. Patsy said of the long note, "Oh, they say that about all the kids."

I just looked at her. "No, they don't. They don't say that about all the kids. This teacher has taken time to write you a very long and thoughtful report. You can't just brush it off."

But she did. We had a big fight about it.

Kitty came to live with us that summer. She never could get to sleep at night. I asked Kitty, real quiet and private in her room, why she couldn't get to sleep. And she said, "Trippy"—which is what she called me— "Trippy, if I go to sleep at night maybe I won't wake up in the morning."

One of the worst things she did to herself was wash her hands fifty times a day. She washed the skin right off her hands. Everything was dirty. She was a fanatic about it. She'd take something like a pencil and ask me if each part was dirty. She'd hold it right up in my face and go from the eraser to the point—"Is this part dirty? Is *this* part dirty?" We couldn't go to a restaurant or a show or anything. She'd suddenly disappear, and we'd find her in the ladies' room with a bar of soap, all lathered up, scrubbing away. And her mother not dealing with it. Kitty couldn't eat at the table with us; she had to have all her food cut up into bite-size pieces and eat silently off in a corner on a TV tray.

Meanwhile, I am getting these calls from Ohio, from the father's girlfriend. She was mad because he kept telling Kitty she was Daddy's Best Girl, his Number-One Girl, and she always would be. The grown-up girlfriend said they had no sex life at all, her and him, because he was so wrapped up in his daughter. I'm just staring at the ceiling and wondering why *I* am hearing this. I got no business with the girlfriend of the father of the daughter of the woman I love. I hated those conversations.

Kitty went to a slumber party for a little friend's birthday, and she and her mother spent the whole day downtown picking out tasteful little gifts and a flowery basket to carry them in. I said to Patsy, "Why aren't you preparing her? She can't go to sleep here, with both of us working on it. How's she going to do it with half a dozen other little girls giggling in the dark?" And sure enough, the calls from the girl's mother started around 11:00 P.M. Patsy would get on the line and talk to Kitty and try to reassure her, but finally along about 2:30 we had to get up and drive down there and get her. Patsy said it was the mother's fault for taking them to *Snow White*—Kitty was frightened by the witch. But that was not what Kitty was frightened of. I'd stare at her raw little hands.

These uncontrollable rages would suddenly possess her. I came in one day and found them on the stairs. Patsy is in tears on the lower stair, and Kitty is standing

on the upper stair just slapping her mother and screaming, her face red as a beet, "Pig shit, pig shit, pig shit." I
separated the combatants and picked up Kitty in my one
arm and put my other arm around her mother. I walked
around the living room with them and said I just couldn't
stand it, to see my two girls this way.

I loved Kitty. She was real special. Smart as a whip.
Beautiful, like her mother, with that long, flowing blond
hair, almost white, way down her little back. We went for
a week to a cottage Patsy rented on the Jersey shore. Kitty
would not set foot into the water; she was much too
messed up and terrified. But late one afternoon, burnt to
a crisp, I was walking back with all our stuff. I had beach
chairs and towels and sand pails and beach balls just
hanging all over me. I was walking way down by the
water, and I didn't look behind me, and a big wave came
in and knocked me down, sent things flying every which
way and covered me over. And here comes Kitty, who
had not set a toe in the water, she came splashing right
in—"Oh, *Trippy!*"—and tried to drag me to my feet, not
thinking for a second of her own safety. She was a tip-top
little girl.

But in such pain. Not a moment's rest. I said she
clearly had to get professional help, it was way too deep
for us. Her mother made an appointment with a child
psychiatrist, but Kitty didn't like her, so they quit. I
thought Patsy could use counseling, but she wouldn't go.
She was probably afraid what she'd find out.

So gradually we drifted apart. Patsy sold her business, and they moved to Syracuse. It was very, very hard
for me to say good-bye. Patsy was the most beautiful
woman I had ever been with. I'd think about her all day
long, and at night I could not get enough of her. It was

the strongest sexual bond of my whole life. Judy—Judy Cook, our dispatcher—once said to me that Patsy was just my plaything. That's not true at all. Judy Cook lets all of us officers know what she thinks about our arrested development. Sexually, policemen do tend to be a little crude. The other officers love to rib Judy; because they know it's a sore spot with her, they go out of their way to indulge in locker-room talk around her. She fumes. But it hurt me when Judy talked to me so scornfully about my feelings for Patsy. They were much more complicated than what Judy thought. I glance through Dick's *Playboys*, and I do not find the playmates all that enticing. Their eyes so empty and dumb. Their boobs are too much of a good thing. But I do not feel the way Judy Cook does about the physical side. I never yet met a lover, of whatever sexual preference, who does not want to be considered beautiful or handsome by the person they love. And that's the way I felt about Patsy. At night on our bed in the moonlight I had died and gone to heaven.

And it wasn't only that. It was everything else about Patsy, too. She loved to dance. We hardly missed a Saturday night out at the Golden Garter. Golf, horseback riding, tramping through the woods. I could hardly keep up with her. She was terrific to get drunk with, put me under the table many a night. Real brassy. I thought nothing could break her spirit. That's why it so took me by surprise with Kitty. The only thing I ever saw Patsy defeated by. She just wouldn't deal with it. Like at the very beginning with that report card. Absolutely would not admit what was staring her right in the face.

So I quit. I couldn't stand losing Patsy. And I dearly loved Kitty. I could have lived with the condition Kitty was in, if only I could have gotten Patsy to cooperate and do something about it. Kitty would go out of her way to think of terrible names for her mother; she gave her no respect at all. She'd make faces at her behind her back, little signals to me that I would refuse to accept. I think it was Kitty's own pathetic little way of crying for help. She was saying, Mommy, I can't live like this, and you're not helping.

They came back to town for a month last summer. One scorching day for old time's sake I went along with them to the Plunge. The three of us were sitting on a bench down by the diving boards watching all the kids take their turns. There was this one skinny blond boy, all vain the way boys that age can be, and he was doing flips and gainers; he was already excellent. Patsy got excited and said he'd be just right as a boyfriend for Kitty. I was very upset at Kitty's physical appearance, she'd dyed her beautiful hair brown, and combed it all over on one side, wearing these big earrings and bracelets. Boy crazy. I thought of this phrase in Ann Landers that the worst consequence of child abuse is the "theft of their innocence." This is true. I looked at Kitty and I thought to myself, Pregnant at sixteen. And here was her mother encouraging it.

Patsy went and talked to the lifeguard and came pitty-pattying barefoot back, in this gorgeous purple bikini, and she said to her daughter, "It's just perfect, pumpkin, he's twelve, too. Why don't you go talk to him?"

And Kitty said, real fast, "If he's so perfect, why don't you go fuck him yourself?"

Took my breath away. Everything got real still on

our bench. I looked at Patsy, and it was like she had been slapped hard in the face. But did she say anything? No, she just sat there, stunned. Finally she looked at me, and I know what the expression on my face was. My look said, Well, I see that things have not gotten any better.

But I can blame Patsy all I want to. I still return to me. I quit. I didn't want the burden. Why couldn't I have just lived with it? Maybe Patsy couldn't help it; maybe she had no way of fixing things. I should have said, Okay, no matter what, we'll weather it, we'll live through it, and I will be here as long as it takes. But I quit. It made my days too difficult. I'd come home from working a shift full of problems, and I didn't want to have to start up at home. Especially since no progress was being made. I kept asking myself what should be done. And I kept coming up blank. It just killed me to see that little girl suffer. To this day I tell myself that maybe I could have fixed it. Just by giving her security and steady routine. But I didn't really believe I could. I feel so guilty about it, I think of myself as One Who Cannot Be Counted On.

But if I had it to do over, I know I'd do the same thing again. It wasn't too much trouble—it was not being able to get Patsy to deal with it. Both mother and daughter adored Dickie. We could have been a family. I guess it was pretty hard on Dickie. He didn't know what was going on; he just knew that every day was devoted to Kitty's problems to the exclusion of all else. We never could do what we had planned. But when "the girls" were gone, he really missed them.

I don't know. The whole thing hangs over me like a shroud.

When I come on my shift, I inherit a problem from the previous officer. Two tires and a car battery have been stolen at one of the apartments in the Carriage House. Then we get a follow-up call that the thefts are more extensive, a lawnmower, gas cans, a couple of bicycles, bags of rock salt. Some guy is down there right now, and he is arguing that the stuff belongs to him. So I hop to it. But by the time I get there the guy has already disappeared. I get a good description of him, and in a matter of minutes I catch up with him trudging down the road muttering to himself and wildly gesturing to the empty air. He says he was just cleaning up junk, he didn't steal anything. He seems to fancy himself a Good Samaritan. He stinks like a bastard; who knows when he had his last bath? He says he can show me all the stolen property. He tells me that he'll be glad to, he can take me right to it if I want. So he climbs into the patrol car and directs me down to the flats, a pretty seedy part of town where people eventually end up when they are down on their luck.

Way back in a little wooded area, this house trailer is surrounded by junk car parts, old rusted swing sets, garbage, tons of garbage. We go into the trailer and he says, "Excuse the mess." Excuse the mess? Hefty garbage

bags overflowing, stacks of dirty pots and pans and dishes
and blankets and boxes of crap everywhere on the
couches and tables and chairs, you can't sit down, you
can hardly walk around. The stench is overpowering. A
lot of dog shit. There's a small room, a kids' bedroom.
No furniture in there—apparently they just crawl into it
like a rat's nest to sleep. Three little dogs running
around, and in the bathroom the tub is full of clothes
covered with mud, and there's a pink potty chair overflowing with shit. Any child who tried to use it would
have to sit right in their own mess. The top is off the
toilet and everything has run all over the sides. The floor
around it is rotted out so that you can see right through
to the bare ground below. They'd pulled the end of the
trailer off and built this small room which is full of tires
and car parts and garbage cans and bottles. Bugs crawling
everywhere, roaches and flies from the dog shit, and
human shit too. The guy makes himself a sandwich, asks
me if I'd like a bite to eat too, and I decline graciously.
Four little kids come in from playing outside. They're
filthy, with food on their faces and tangled hair, a small
one with a diaper that hasn't been changed recently,
sores on them, bad teeth when they smile. They'd be
cute kids if you'd take 'em through a car wash and get
the crud off them. I see I have got to call the child
protective agency.

Their father keeps mumbling about taking a lie
detector test. He works as a cook somewhere—I wish I
knew the restaurant he cooks at. I advise him of his
rights and tell him he'll have to give up his habit of just
grabbing things that aren't nailed down and do not belong
to him. On the way back to the station the smell coming

off him is so strong that I have to roll the windows down, even though it's freezing cold. He hasn't bathed in months. He's talking crazy, doesn't know what he is saying. He keeps insisting he is only involved in one part of this, he didn't steal anything. I tell him the children may have to be taken away, I wouldn't treat my dog like that. At the station the other officer snickers a bit; he'd already seen the trailer. I fingerprint our subject and photograph him, and he wants to make a statement. He skips from subject to subject. I read it back to him and have him initial the places where it makes no sense at all. Frankly I would like to slap the piss out of him. A bar of soap costs twenty-three cents, a half a can of beer. After I run him up to the jail, I take a long shower. I'm itching all over with bugs and fleas, probably in my imagination, but I can't get the smell out of my nose.

When I get off duty, tired and out of sorts, I stop in to check with ol' Sydney. I need a lift. Her world is a welcome relief from the shit-load of mine. And she does not fail me. It's the difference between night and day. Her apartment is full of cigarette smoke, and I crack open the window in the kitchen. She's in an old brown fuzzy bathrobe; she's been slaving away all day on her doctor's dissertation. She can't get a chapter right.

"What," I ask, "seems to be the problem?" As if I would know one single thing about it.

She says she's been working on it far longer than she should. A big wastebasket is overflowing with papers, full ashtrays all around this big electric typewriter.

She shows me. And, as we go through it, I can hardly believe that this sort of thing would actually be a person's job. But I guess that's the point. You don't judge it by the real world. It's the midnight oil burning in the tippy-top window of the ivory tower.

The first thing she plops in front of me is a page in this book called *Long Day's Journey into Night*. It's the last act of the play, and this young guy Edmund is arguing with his father late at night, while playing cards. They both seem to have been drinking. Edmund is telling about when he was a sailor. Edmund goes ape-shit about the calm sea and the gentle rocking of the ship. I read it, and I figure I understand it pretty much. Edmund is quite the fellow. Then Sydney takes that book away from me, and she hands me *Moby-Dick* by Herman Melville, which I have always been meaning to read. Sydney opens this book to chapter 35, "The Mast-Head," and it's the exact same deal: boy in crow's nest, calm sea, rocking boat. O'Neill's Edmund is just like Melville's boy.

I say, "That's interesting, catching O'Neill with his hand in the cookie jar."

"What?"

I say, "Well, he stole it, right? Plagiarized it?"

She looks at me kind of strangely.

I say, "I got caught doing that once. In high school I copied an article out of the encyclopedia. My big mistake was copying down, 'See Illustration, facing page.' "

She smiles at me. She says, "No, the problem here is figuring out exactly how it works. Did O'Neill hold *Moby-Dick* open beside him while he was writing Edmund's speech? Did he do it from memory? Or what?"

I study it again. I go back and forth between them and get mixed up about which is which.

I read over what she has written. Looks fine to me. I say, "Nobody's ever noticed this before?"

She stands up kind of swaggery, and she says, "One hesitates to rush into print with common knowledge." She goes and gets us more coffee. I am pretty totally in the dark. I know nothing about the value of such things. I am a bit amazed, though, to compare the different days that the two of us have had. She's been holed up here going back and forth between Eugene O'Neill and Herman Melville while I've been bandying about with a foul kleptomaniac.

I can see how much of herself she puts into it. Smoking all day, not stopping to eat. And I think of how she was over at the college, marching to and fro in front of the big white screen after *On the Waterfront*. Getting her ideas across to all the kids. I've never met a woman like this.

When I finally am able to tear myself away, I am very careful, I'd hate to spoil anything. She probably thinks of me just as this funny cop who was nice to her. Which is just who I am. I will leave it at that.

Still, I don't go home. I drive around aimlessly for a while, not exactly thinking, just sort of feeling things like you do when you're a kid and wonder if your feelings for a girl are in any way reciprocated. You wonder if it gives her pleasure to think of you. Man, the way she talked about those two different boys in the crow's nest. Or whatever it was. I still don't see why you can't just say O'Neill stole it. It's right down there in black and white. But I guess you don't exactly "steal" words and ideas, not like the Jack of All Filth stole bikes and bags of rock salt.

We have this freakish little spell of warm weather. The snow melts. It is almost what you could call balmy. On a quiet Sunday night around nine o'clock, a lady calls in to report she can hear a kid yelling on her neighbor's roof. I respond down to the address. It's a big house with a slate roof, several peaks, and up on the third story is this little face looking out over a gable. I yell up to the boy to relax and hang on and stay there. He has apparently climbed out of his bedroom window and gone exploring on the roof; when the sun went down, the slate got slick because the dew formed on it, and there he sits. I look the situation over. I realize I have to tell the dispatcher to call the fire department and bring down the ladder truck. I get on the radio, and then I wait and talk to the kid. He really wants to get down, he is a little upset. Pretty soon the truck arrives, manned by a bunch of volunteer firemen, and of course they have their red lights on and the siren going. Neighbors come out. A crowd forms, and we have this whole group of people watching us. The truck backs up over the sidewalk into the front yard. It takes three tries to get up over the curb, because the grass is wet and the tires spin. It makes some pretty deep ruts in the lawn. The ladder is thirty feet long and extends another twenty feet, so we have enough reach. At the top of the ladder there's this big bucket you can stand in. They turn spotlights on the house—it looks like a real professional operation. A fireman starts up the ladder, and the boy on the roof starts screaming, no, he wants the policeman. So I get stuck with the great honor of climbing this freaking ladder to get the boy off the roof.

The kid is only about six or seven years old. He has a pair of Doctor Dentons on, no slippers, blood all over his hands and bare feet and on the front of his little outfit. He has cut himself on the tin flashing of the slate roof. I get him in the bucket with me, and they lower us down. We have a tense moment when we descend between some electric lines. About halfway down the little guy turns to me and says, "You see that big tree over there?" And I see this humongous oak tree in the side yard, with a thousand limbs on it. The boy says, "I'd really like to climb to the top of that tree someday and see what's up there." I think to myself, You little bastard, you better stay on the ground, you get to the top of that tree and you'll never get down. But he is serious, he really wants to climb that tree. He probably will someday, and I'll have to take him out of it. We get him down on the ground, and the baby-sitter, a fifteen-year-old girl, is beside herself. We look the boy's injuries over, and they're not too bad. We take him into the house and wash him up. The first-aid guys from the fire department put some Band-Aids on him and straighten him up. I talk to the next-door lady, the one who called, and she says this little guy is into everything. Now that he's safe, his mouth is running a mile a minute. It seems to excite him to see his blood on my uniform.

Next day the father calls. Not to thank us. He's pissed off about the ruts in his lawn.

I do a little halfhearted studying for the lieutenant's exam. I failed it once already, three years ago, so I am not too optimistic this time. They have several study courses you can take, but I never seem to have the time. I don't tell Dick about it, because I don't want to have to tell him when I fail again. I certainly do not mention it to my newfound friend, Sydney. Which is probably a mistake—she could help me with the English parts of it. I am not strong in vocabulary. I sit there staring at the page a long time when I come across one of their little zingers:

> To refer to the "proximate cause" of an accident is
> the same as referring to the
> A. possible cause
> B. probable cause
> C. principal cause
> D. presumed cause
> E. palpable cause

I just hate those buggers—and cannot seem to leave them behind me once they get under my skin. I do not have the sense to go with my first instinct, which is usually right. I always come back and erase and circle another. I get all balled up, looking for tricks:

> Which of the following types of evidence can justify
> the inference of the existence of a litigated fact even
> though it does not actually prove a fact?
> A. Prima facie evidence
> B. Circumstantial evidence

C. Conclusive evidence
D. Primary evidence
E. Corroboratory evidence

I fail to see what this has to do with actual police work. Vocabulary niceties are not on your mind when you are into nuts-and-bolts matters. If I were to ask Sydney's help, I would feel too much at a disadvantage. She knows all about writing and creativity and English. I know how to be a policeman. We belong to two separate worlds. My mind always comes back to that when I get to daydreaming about how pretty she is.

I do not consider myself stupid. I do know I am uneducated to a great degree. When you are a police officer, you control the situation. You're the one doing the talking, and everybody else listens. They may try to talk over your head, but you know your field. Most policemen, if they are any good, can read people. Quickly. You can size them up and know which way to go, whether to be lenient and understanding or whether to trap them. You sharpen your instincts. You can tell almost immediately whether this guy is bullshitting you or being truthful. You listen for the complexity of his story. You listen for holes. But Sydney talks to me about stuff I have never even heard of. I realize there is a lot out there that I haven't even tasted or been exposed to. Sydney knows things which I do not have the foggiest notion of. She has much greater background. I talk with her and I see I am on shaky ground. My conversation gets confused. It's like I am the criminal telling the story and she's the policeman.

It intimidates me to the point that sometimes I am

even afraid to leave her a note. She likes us to leave notes. She does not realize I am painfully aware of the mistakes I may make. When you write a police report, you can be real simple, the simpler the better, the easier for everybody to understand. But when I write a note to her, I sit down and get all uneasy. When she writes one to me, like "I am lonely for your purty face," I first of all notice that my heart skips a beat and maybe the ideas I have brewing are not merely my own one-sided insanity. I also notice the way she spells "pretty," and know she does it that way to be affectionate, but I can't spell worth dink. And my sentences do not run together like hers do; mine connect very poorly. So I leave her notes because she enjoys it, but if I were in charge, I wouldn't. I used to write letters, just dash them off. Not anymore. I hate to look stupid.

And now it is not confined to writing. I can hardly talk, so conscious am I of what I do not know. For years I have talked to doctors and lawyers, but I always keep it on my plane. You can do that as a policeman because you have the authority to stop the conversation at any time and take action. When you stop an intellectual, you control the situation. You have him on your turf. He is out of his element. If I were to go to him as a teacher, then he would be calling the shots and would basically do the same thing to me as I am doing now to him. And with Sydney I am frequently out of the water. I try to act more intelligent than I am. I know who should rule India or Pakistan. Of course, my arguments are all full of holes. I know enough not to try brain surgery, but with Sydney I feel this spirit of competition. I become aggressive. I forget to stick to what I know.

Most policemen, if they are honest about the matter, are intimidated by an intellectual. That is why there is always a lot of tension between the cops and the college students. A policeman knows that most of these kids are brighter than he is. They have had more exposure to world travel and the finer things in life. The cop is dredging along—he is not going to the New York City Ballet; he is not traveling to Europe; he is not flying to the Bahamas over spring vacation. That is all part of the problem you have between the police and certain segments of society. I try to treat everybody the same, but I realize I have gut feelings, not knowledge. When it comes to police work, I know what I am doing. I've been in it long enough. I know what has to be done, I know how to get it done. Whenever possible, I use my head instead of my nightstick. You can convince people, compromise them, defuse them. Sydney does not really talk down to me. She tries to raise me up a bit. Sometimes she makes me uncomfortable. I try to make light of the differences between us, but I cannot handle the feeling of inadequacy.

I show up along with six other candidates at the basement of the courthouse for the lieutenant's exam. I breeze right through the first dozen or so questions. I am all confidence. This time I shall pass. The exam seems to have a different complexion from the first one. I am charging away. It is practical:

> The use of a roadblock is simply an adaptation to police practices of the military concept of encirclement. Successful operation of a roadblock plan depends almost entirely on the amount of advance

study and planning given to such operations. A thorough and detailed examination of the roads and terrain and jurisdiction of the police agency shall be made with the location of the roadblock pinpointed in advance. The first principle to be borne in mind in the location of each roadblock is the time element. Its location must be at a point beyond which the fugitive could not have traveled between the time elapsed from the commission of the crime and the arrival of the officers at the roadblock.

I am whipping through it, waiting for the multiple choice questions to test my reading comprehension. But when I turn the page of the big examination booklet I just stare:

Internal management reporting in government agencies is becoming more statistical in nature. Statistics have thus become a major tool of management supervision in public agencies. Before deciding to adopt statistical reporting as a management tool, the management of a public agency should first determine whether the
  A. employees of the agency understand the need for and use of statistics in reporting
  B. supervisory staff in the agency is capable of putting reports in statistical form
  C. major activities of the agency can be reported statistically
  D. present achievements of the agency can be reported statistically as a comparison with previous years

Reports submitted to the department heads should be completed to the last detail. As far as possible, summaries should be avoided. This statement is in general
  A. correct only on the basis of information complete so that a decision can be reached

B. not correct; if all the reports were of this
   character a department head could never complete his work
C. correct; the decision as to what is important
   or not can only be made by a person who is
   responsible for the action
D. not correct; preliminary reports obviously
   cannot be complete to the last detail
E. correct; summaries tend to conceal the exact
   state of affairs and to encourage generaliza-
   tions which would not be made if the details
   were known, and consequently should be
   avoided.

What happened to my roadblock? I cannot make
head or tails of this statistics shit. Albany must have
screwed up the exam format. We got a monitor, this
prune-faced lady, so I clear my throat and raise my hand.
She trudges on these air-sole shoes to my desk, and I
show her the problem. We whisper away, and she says,
"Just do the best you can." I say, Maybe the other men
have this problem too. She whispers that nobody else has
complained. I think maybe they haven't got to this part
yet. We fuss and jabber, and finally she just walks back to
the front. But now I have lost all my confidence. I am out
of sorts. Now the questions make no sense to me at all. I
am angry.

One of the following which is not an integrated
element of a report system or work measurement is
   A. a uniform record form for accumulating data
      and instructions for its maintenance
   B. procedures for routing reports upward in the
      organization and routing summaries down-
      ward

C. a standard report form for summarizing basic records and instructions for its preparation
D. a method of summarizing, analyzing, and presenting data from several reports
E. a loose-leaf manual which contains all procedural material which is reasonably permanent and has a substantial reference value

I am reading the answers aloud in my head, in this pompous voice, making fun of phrases like "substantial reference value." I am very scornful now, not concentrating on finding what they are looking for. I realize that once again I am going to fail. Toward the end of the four hours I finally find my roadblock questions, on the back of that page, and I answer them without referring to the paragraph they go with. I read, "D. If the method of escape is not known, it should be assumed that it is by automobile." I say in my head, No, they got choppers. I say, No, they hop aboard a bus. I am not really thinking. My asshole is killing me after sitting so long on a hard chair. I sneeze all over my answer sheet, and I laugh out loud as I daub around with my hanky, smearing my answers in my number-2 pencil. When prune-face calls time, I stomp out totally demoralized. I get into 1 GROUCH and swing by Sydney's. She's not there. I don't leave a note.

But after a couple of bad days, during which I am real pissy, my sunny disposition reasserts itself. I realize that with Sydney and me the attraction is mutual. Now the pressure is building up, and the day of reckoning is near. We're jumpy around each other, it is so much on both our minds. Each is waiting for the other to make the first move.

And then it happens. Two people who do not travel in the same circles at all have nevertheless been drawn together to the ultimate point. One day I stop by her apartment after I get off duty at three, and we dawdle a bit over coffee, hardly talking. The feeling is so powerful I can hardly lift my cup to my lips, I am shaking so bad. Or so it seems to me. She sits down beside me. One hand is in a cast, but she runs the other one along my arm. I look at her. She sees I have received her message. Unless, of course, I have lost my mind. But her eyes are so lively, and she has this heightened color in her face. When the phone rings, we both jump a foot. She goes and gets it, and says to whoever it is, "Look, I can't talk now, I'll call you back." A couple of times she says, "Yes, yes," laughing. In my mind I make up the person she's talking to, a woman friend of hers, who must know her pretty well. She has told this friend about me, and the friend has guessed I am here right now, and guessed what we are about to do. Again, I wonder if I have gone crazy. She comes over and stands next to me. She touches me again, on the shoulder this time, and her touch is so gentle and soft. I sit here looking up at her. If I am wrong about what is going on here, I should not be allowed to wander loose on the streets. Finally, she takes me by the hand, this real serious little smile on her face. She leads me into her bedroom. She lets go of my hand and touches her fingers to my face.

The first time, you're so new to each other. You don't know each other's signals. And this is more than that because I am afraid of hurting her, given what her last experience ended up doing to her. Even without that, I'd want to give her plenty of time. So I am as gentle as I know how to be. Which is not the easiest thing in the world. Paramount in my mind, almost paramount, is the desire to reassure her.

After, we lie here for a long time in the winter afternoon. We both kind of drop off, though I don't see how I really could do so, since I watch her sleep.

I can't say about other men, but the first time for me is always a bit difficult. I'm fearful of presenting myself badly. Sometimes I have trouble getting it up, which infuriates me half to death because how is the woman supposed to know the problem is the opposite of what it looks like? I remember as a teenager one time I got to the land of my dreams with this girl, and just as I was on the way in, I belched. Jesus Christ. If you've already done it a few times and have gotten used to each other, and trust each other, a belch is no big deal. But even when things go without incident, you almost always feel, afterward, that it has been too abrupt.

Syd and I arrange our schedules so that we have lots of time. Talk in bed after. Have soup and crackers.

We go to this real late movie downtown on the Commons, and when we return to the car, it's the only one still there. We had parked in Woolworth's big lot, under a tall silver-white light. We get into the front seat, and these big soft flakes of snow start to fall on the windshield. The wind tosses the snowflakes so that they kind of lift up before they come in for a landing. Syd makes up a foolish little story about a lost tribe of homeless snowflakes. At first I'm afraid she's serious, but then I see she's being a wise-ass. We get to laughing.

And then kissing. And then really kissing. Before we know what we're about, we've unzipped this and unbuttoned that and pulled up this and pulled down that, and we're doing it right in the front seat of the car. I'm waiting for a brother officer to tap his flashlight on the window and say, "Hey, kids, they've invented houses for that."

The lost tribe of homeless snowflakes has completely covered the windshield; we're in our own private world like a cave. Finally I get out and brush off the snow. I look down, and under my hand is her face up real close to the glass, like a little kid's face.

Next day when I come by her apartment, she calls out, "Is that you?" and I say it is, and she says, "Come in, it's open," and I find her in the bedroom stark naked except for a little blue visored cap with "Jr. Police" printed on it in yellow. Bought at Woolworth's.

I get switched over to graveyard, and it comes time for her to be introduced to my house. She seems to like it okay for a place which nowhere has a woman's touch. She's still there one afternoon when Dick comes home from school. You can see he's pretty shocked, Sydney's closer to his age than mine.

The entire sexual field continues to perplex me. Back there in the fifties, when I was Dick's age, sex was dirty. Forbidden. All we had was rubbers; the pill hadn't even been invented yet. So there was this overwhelming fear of pregnancy. Which meant that we'd do everything *but*. We couldn't take the strain, and half the kids in my graduating class got married within the year, out of sheer horniness. Some of my classmates are grandparents now.

I myself am beginning to show my age. For the last

five or six years I have been a bundle of aches and pains.
All my previous life I took my body for granted. It never
failed me. Recently, however, my body is like a car that
serves you well and then suddenly everything starts to
fall apart at once, you can hardly drive it, it's always in
the shop. My asshole never gives me a moment's peace,
throbbing and burning all the time. I have trouble just
getting in and out of the cruiser. I eat like a horse, but
none of it stays with me. I'm down fifteen pounds. At
night I wake up soaked with perspiration and can hardly
find a dry place on the sheets to go back to sleep. Which
is why Sydney and I have not once slept together through
a night. I'm embarrassed. I do not want her to know what
an ordeal the night is for me. It's why I do not mind so
much taking my turn on graveyard. I don't sweat so much
when I only got time for catnaps in the day. And you
hurt yourself a lot in this job, you're always getting cuts
and bruises. Mine take forever to heal.

Sydney, being Jewish, has a frank and open attitude.
Jewish girls seem to me warmer than most. Probably
because there is a lot of touching and cuddling in the
family setting. As opposed to the stiffness of the silent
majority. Once I went with a real pretty Catholic girl,
and the nuns had taught her sex was dirty, and she was
quite out of touch with her desires. Sydney, however, is
right at home. She knows what she wants and she goes
after it. Not hectic, just a serious lady who has thought
about it, as her profession makes thinking natural for her
to do. I suspect she would not have had much use for me
when I was her age. I was fucking everything I could lay
my hands on, so proud of fucking a lot of women, when
in reality I was only fucking myself. Pretty shallow. It's

probably even a good thing that I am so much older now. If I were like I was in the old days, I'd be finished and up and dressed by the time that now we are just making our way into the main course. I want different things. Like her eyes. At her age I was just taking aerial photographs of the landscape below. But when we really get to the mountaintop, I'm eighteen again, as young and hungry as I've ever been. You want it to go on forever and never stop till you die. All the bullshit and sorrow and shabbiness of the world I have known as a policeman seems to drop away.

Now, sitting in the patrol car at 2:00 A.M., I think of Sydney. I get big in my pants and relive the big event of the day, step by step, slowly, pausing over each detail, no matter how small. Sometimes it's one of the smallest that makes me sigh.

Wayne Parker, one of our younger officers, is only about five seven, but he must weigh 230, and he moves around in the world like this squat little tank. He is a Vietnam veteran, saw a lot of action over there; his legs are all shot to hell, and he gets disability from the federal government. He chatters constantly. The worst part is that he doesn't know truth from nontruth. He makes up stories. I trust him as far as I can throw him. Makes me nervous. He's had about three wives. Does his job, at least on the day shifts, but you never know whether he's telling the truth or not. You have to filter out the truth from the way he embellishes everything. Sometimes you know for a fact that he's telling you bullshit. You keep it to yourself when he tells you something that you know it is impossible for him to have done. The worst part of it is that he's like the little boy who cried wolf. Someday he's going to come on the air and need help and nobody's going to pay any attention to him. I've been on the air with him when he was on a high-speed chase, and there was no chase, he was just stirring things up. Not good. Not good.

But this is not all that is wrong with Wayne Parker. You try to make allowances for a man with a Purple Heart, but when he's working graveyard, he comes on at eleven, walks beat for an hour, and then goes over to the fire station and falls asleep on the couch. Whoever else is on duty has to handle all the incoming calls. I guess he's exhausted—he has a part-time job as an electrician during the day. Once at 2:00 A.M. we decided to mess with him a little bit because we were so mad at having to do his work for him. We got about two hundred feet of rope and tied one end of it to the leg of the couch, and then all five of us got on the other end of the rope and started running, we jerked his ass right off the couch. He comes walking into the station house with the rope. He was pissed bright red. Wouldn't speak to anybody for a couple of days.

All it did was change his sleep habits. He'd go all the way to the end of some garages out on North Forest, hide back there, and go to sleep in the backseat of the patrol car. What we mischief makers did that time was activate the siren by mashing down the horn ring with masking tape, then turn the siren on and run. It took him five minutes to get out of the backseat and stop it, all around the neighborhood the lights going on.

So one day he gets fed up. Several of us are standing around in the station when he gets off duty after busting his balls for eight hours. He picks on me, since I have kind of been the ringleader in all of the dirty tricks. He shouts at me, "I've had enough, Triphammer, you son of a bitch, you have fucked with me for the last time!" He whips a revolver out of his locker, an old Colt .45 army issue, and he slams the locker door, and he steps right up to me and shoots me. I think I am dead—I have always thought this is the way it will happen to me, point-blank. But not from a brother officer. I look down for the blood

because the concussion from the blank in the gun makes
this *thud* on my shirt.

The other guys say I turned white as a sheet. I was
absolutely speechless. Wayne thinks it is a really neat
trick. I don't. I go out and drive around for a while before
heading home. I stop at Sydney's, but she's over at school.
So I pick up a load of dry cleaning and do some grocery
shopping. I'm trying to calm myself down. I get no help
in that job when I pull into our driveway. Dick's blue
Chevy is sitting there with the fender all crumpled in,
the same fender as before. I find Dick in his room, and
he can't seem to focus on the fact that this shit costs
money and is a big nuisance. The other vehicle involved
is a Volkswagen Rabbit convertible, belonging to this kid
named Aaron whose father is a big shot psychology
professor at the college. Aaron was horsing around and
hit him just as he was pulling out of the high school
parking lot. The damage was more extensive to Aaron's
car, all along the panels on the passenger side. Dick sits
there sucking on a pencil and not looking me in the eye.
There is more here than is coming out. But Dick doesn't
want to go into it. So I figure the best thing is to let the
two boys work it out themselves.

Which only gets us to the middle of dinner. Aaron's
father calls, he says he is worried about two "apparent
contradictions" in the situation thus far. I know this sort
of bird; he uses big fancy language to intimidate people
and make them feel foolish in the presence of his awe-
some intellect. I tell him to calm down. He thinks he can
bulldoze a cop who only went to high school. He says
that there would "indeed" be no police report if his son
had not filed one. This contradicts what Dick told me.

Dick said he didn't want to tattle, and since Aaron was at fault, he, Dick, wanted to let Aaron file the report. Aaron said he would do it after getting his wits about him at his girlfriend's house for an hour, and then call back. But Aaron never called back. The professor says that "an additional matter of concern" to him was that Dick was the one who suggested that they say Aaron hit Dick's car while it was stationary in the parking lot. Dick says it was Aaron's suggestion. I guess there had been more back-and-forth telephone calls than Dick had told me. After I bid the professor a fond farewell, I sit down with Dick. I say I can't help you if you don't tell me the truth.

And then he does tell me. He says Aaron is a pretty messed-up kid. Lots of emotional problems. All Aaron cares about is his rock band. And he's really into drugs. He's stoned in class. And he's dealing dope at the school; he sells pot to Erik. I'm pretty miffed when I hear all this. I want to call the professor back and give him a piece of what I call my mind. I want to say to him, Wake up and smell the coffee—your son's a drug dealer. How are you handling the matter? How do you expect your boy to conquer his drug problems and be a man in this world if Daddy is always running interference for him? Then I have this little burst of pride for Dick when he finally confesses that Aaron was stoned when the accident occurred, stoned out of his skull. Which explains why Dick wanted to let him have the time to sober up at the girlfriend's house before he has to go file an accident report. I can't rag on Dick for being irresponsible when what he was doing is kind of softhearted and generous. I

tell him that. He seems relieved. So this second fender
bender has a happier outcome than the first.

Next day at 3:15 I come into the house and Dick
and Becky are here. It's her birthday. I gradually realize
that they want the place to themselves. So I say I'm going
out to do a few errands. I notice Dick has bought her
presents, one of which is this handsome edition of her
favorite book, *Pride and Prejudice*. Dick is mad at some
guy at school, and Becky shakes her head and says, "Yeah,
what an *ass*hole." It startles me to hear this beautiful girl
who loves *Pride and Prejudice* say "*ass*hole."

I say, "Happy birthday." And make myself scarce.

I feel kind of stupid driving aimlessly around the
neighborhood in 1 GROUCH so that those two will feel
free to do unspeakable things. I drive over to Buttermilk
Falls and get out and look down at the frozen gorge. In
my mind's eye I see the yellow ski parka way below on
the ice. I stand here a minute in memory of Scott. I go
have a cigarette in the car and wish Sydney would hurry
up and come back from visiting her parents in New York
City. I contrive to do a little shopping at the A & P.
Finally I cruise on home at a quarter to five and make a
lot of unnecessary noise in the driveway. But the two
lovebirds are fully dressed, drinking tea in the living
room. Dick had invited Becky to dinner, but he forgot
that the indoor soccer championship was today at six. He
has to run to that, and they will have dinner afterward.
As usual, the boy has cut it too close; he has very little
sense of time. So he tears off to the field of battle, and I
drive his girlfriend home. She's wearing a real pretty new
agate necklace Dick seems to have thoughtfully picked
out somewhere. I know he really admires her. He says

she is on top of things. She writes letters to the editor of
the newspaper on subjects like Jews being able to emigrate from the Soviet Union. What young lady of my
generation would ever write a letter to the editor on such
a topic? She's got these beautiful big sloe eyes. If it's any
of my business, I approve of Rebecca for Dick. But it's
none of my business.

That night the lovebirds are off celebrating somewhere. Sydney is still in Manhattan with her family. I
have nothing to do, nothing to stay sober for. So I don't.
I'm disappointed in myself, doing it out of sheer boredom. I prefer an excuse. And Dick comes home before I
hit the hay. I am way too talkative. I can see how distasteful he finds it.

I try to make up for it in the morning. I go out with
a bad hangover and buy us a big bag of fancy doughnuts,
spice-apple and peanut-crunch and cinnamon, to eat
while we watch the Lakers game. But Dick wakes up out
of sorts. I get annoyed with him. Somehow we get on the
subject of college. Finally he has enough of me; he storms
out of the house, gets into his damaged Chevy, and takes
off at a pretty good rate of speed.

I find his glasses on the dining room table. I have
told him he cannot use his car unless he wears his
glasses. So I jump in 1 GROUCH and pick him up two
blocks away. I follow him down to the high school. He
was going to shoot hoops with the guys in the gym. I stop
him on the path. I say, You can express your regrets to
the guys. But I think you will spend today in your room,
catching up on homework. You know you are never to
drive without your glasses. Dick's fuming. He's looking

at me like I am a complete waste of time. I am throbbing at both ends, my head and my asshole.

When he comes back out of the gym, I say for him to drive home and I will follow. Which is what we do. Until we get about halfway there. The road makes a Y, and Dick does not go right, toward home—he suddenly guns her off to the left. And I step on it, I am in hot pursuit.

The first thing Dick does which drives me nuts involves two little kids, a boy and a girl. They're only about five or six years old, standing on opposite sides of the road, all bundled up. They're batting back and forth this white plastic ball with these little yellow plastic racquets. They about piss their pants when the blue Chevy tears past them, and Dick doesn't even slow down. I hit my brakes and crawl by them, this sorry-about-that smile on my face. I resume speed, and now Dick's got quite a lead on me. It takes a while for me to catch up to him again, winding around the virtually deserted streets on Sunday morning. Shit, he's doing fifty in a thirty zone. Our next potential tragedy involves an old geez out walking his two little black dogs. The senior citizen is plodding along like the batteries in his feet have died, the dogs frisky as hell. Dick zooms past them, almost hits one of the dogs, and again I have to come almost to a stop. The elderly gentleman gives me a look of horror; he puts his hands up to the sides of his head. Again, I prop this stupid smile on my face and creep by, then start to go after Dick again, but I ease off the gas and just coast. This is no good. I'm making him crazy. We will have a tragedy if this keeps up. He'll hit someone. Up ahead I see him barrel right through a stop sign.

I go home and sit in the car in the driveway for a
while. I go inside and pace back and forth in the living
room. I have a beer for my hangover. I wonder how long
he'll keep it up, without me on his tail. Surely he will
come to his senses. I picture myself as him, behind the
wheel of the Chevy, and I am simultaneously very frightened and very angry. Then I am me again, wondering
how in all my lessons I have not taught him respect for
the lives of others. My son does not seem to have any
notion at all that an automobile can be a deadly weapon.

I'm on my second beer when the Chevy comes
slowly into the driveway. He gets out with a big bag of
goodies from McDonald's. He shoots me a fuck-you
glance and heads straight for his room. He slams the door
and his boom box comes on with ear-splitting rock music. I sit there for a while, then go to his door. It's locked.
I shout at him to open it. I visualize him in there
crouched in his bed over a quarter-pounder and fries. I
beat the shit out of the door. Finally I go out into the
garage and get a whole bunch of screwdrivers. I come
back and use the biggest one to pry open the door. I really
fuck up the lock and splinter the wood. But he's moved
his dresser over to block the entrance. Then the screaming starts. He screams bloody murder. Huge sounds, not
words, it goes on and on. There's a lot of banging around
in there, like he's throwing himself back and forth off
the walls. And then it stops, except for the boom box;
dead still from Dick, he's screamed himself out.

But it's too quiet. I panic. I think he's hurt himself.
I visualize blood everywhere. I kind of half run back out
to the garage and pull my old rickety stepladder off its
hook. I carry it around to his window, prop it against the

side of the house and climb up and peek in his window. He's lying on his bed like a dead person. I have this hallucination, like I'm inside and looking outside at me, my face in the window. It's very weird. I'm going nuts. I climb back down the stepladder and stand there in the cold. Has he injured his head? I'm shaky as hell.

I go inside and watch the basketball game on TV. I chain smoke and eat two of the fancy doughnuts.

It's half time when Dick comes out. He joins me in the living room. He sits on the couch and neither one of us says anything for a spell. Finally I turn off the TV. I sit back down. I say, "This can't go on."

Dick goes out into the kitchen, and after a bit I follow him and he's not there. I peep out into the garage, and I can't figure it out. I go down to the basement, and he's sitting on a pile of boxes behind the water heater. I say, "You're weird. You're *weird.*"

He stalks upstairs and I follow him. I start in on him about the car.

He says, "I can't help what I feel."

I sit on the black stool by the phone. I say, "You can't help what you feel, but you can help what you do. You didn't even slow down for those little children playing paddleball. Or that old fart walking his little dogs. You can run away from home. But you can't drive away. On foot you won't hurt other people."

He's standing here by the sink, spitting into it.

Then, before I know what is happening, he has his keys out, ready to drive away again. His glasses are nowhere in sight. All of a sudden we are struggling in the open door to the garage, the screen-door kind of banging against us, and I have got him by the hair—I am dragging my son by the hair back into the house, and he is screaming again. I'm hurting him by trying not to hurt him, yanking away with fistfuls of hair.

It is only about the worst day of our life. Black Sunday.

We sit down in the living room, and I tell him the truth. I say, "I miss my little boy. I miss the kid you used to be."

He looks at me.

"When you were a little boy, if I told you to go out in the rain and stand on one leg in the front yard and sing 'Yankee Doodle,' you'd do it."

He says, "I never really did that, did I?"

I say, "I don't see why your growing up has to be based on defying me all the time. Maybe it does. I don't know, I'm a rookie at this. But could we leave the high-speed car chases on TV where they belong?"

He looks away, thinking. And then he turns back to me and nods. The two of us sit in the living room, no lights, darkness coming on. He says in his own defense that he did come home pretty quick, after stopping at McDonald's. He says, "I knew you'd be worried. That shows I think of your feelings."

I grant him that.

He says, "Yeah, but all you did was yell at me."

I grant him that, too. And I make a confession. I say, "Look, I did some high-speed driving when I was your age. A hundred miles an hour. On an empty highway. But I didn't do it in front of my father."

He says he has driven real fast at night too. "And I had passengers," he says. "And I was stoned."

I say, "Jesus, don't do it again."

We are both exhausted. He says softly, "I really want to fix things, Dad. You don't know how much."

I tell him I do.

He sighs and shakes his head and says, "Well, I should hope so."

Dick's off with Becky at a school dance, and Sydney and I are in my den with our after-dinner coffee. It's been a red-letter day for her—today the cast came off her hand. It's a great relief. We sit here just looking at each other. I hope she is thinking what I am thinking. She asks me a question. Now she wants to know about my nickname. "Triphammer" doesn't please her. She says, "Why do you have to name yourself after a part of a gun?"

A part of a gun?

"Well, isn't it, you know, the trigger thing—?"

I kind of laugh. I say, "No, a triphammer isn't a 'trigger thing.' "

"It's not?"

"No, it's a waterfall."

She stares at me. "A waterfall?"

I'm tickled. First I explain to her what a real triphammer is. She can't quite get her female professor mind around levers and cams. "Besides," she says, "what's it got to do with waterfalls?"

Suddenly I remember my little green book. What did I do with that? I think it's somewhere down in the basement. A few years ago, when we were on friendlier terms, Judy Cook gave me that book for my birthday. I

think once when I was mad at her I put it in the basement. Childish. But now I say to Sydney, "Excuse me a
minute. I'll show you something about triphammers."

I go down into the basement, and I rummage around.
I find it right where I put it, beside the empty fish tank
that I had set up in Dick's room when he was ten years
old. I finally gave up on that goddamn fish tank; in the
morning it was so depressing to find guppies belly-up on
the surface. But here's my little green book from Judy
Cook. I dust it off and go back upstairs to my den. I show
it to Syd. It's an old guide book to this upstate area,
published in 1866, just one year after the Civil War. It's
written in that crazy fancy talk they used back then. I
show Sydney the paragraph, and she reads it aloud. She
gets into the spirit and gives it a lot of expression: " 'The
echo of the opposite cliff is truly stunning. It deepens
and more than doubles the roar of the cataract, which
from this regular and answering beat is called "Triphammer Falls." ' "

That "Triphammer Falls" takes her by surprise, she
lets out a little laugh. She stops and stares at the page.
For the next part she makes her voice kind of all mock
serious: " 'Alas, wretched mortal that I am, here I attempt to show off Nature's glories as if they were calico
patterns. You will return from hence a wearier but a
wiser and I trust a better mortal.' "

Her eyes run ahead of her voice again, and she seems
to like the writing in this part because she reads it slow:
" 'The Cyclopean hammers are ringing with response, a
Duet of Floods. The waters come winding and gliding
through the narrowing pass until they plunge over the

precipice in an amber stream; they strike upon the opposing rock, rebounding in the wildest foam.' "

"Not bad," she says, "not bad at all. Hudson River School."

She gets up and comes over to where I am sitting. She stands between my legs and holds the book flat open in her hands like a piece of music. She sort of proclaims it: " 'Do not be afraid. Woo Nature boldly. Stand now directly in the presence of the mighty Triphammer!' "

I am grinning. I lock my knees on her legs. I say, "Calm yourself."

She looks down at me. "Calm myself? When I am standing directly in the presence of the mighty Triphammer?"

I tell her that I grew up just a stone's throw from it. My mother used to take me there to play when I was little. I'd just keep tugging at her, "Twiphamma, Twiphamma!" It's my favorite place in the world. At the base of the falls the water hits the rocks and makes this big hollow bubble, and you can get inside it and breathe, water all around you. When I was a kid, I'd climb in and never come out.

Syd says, "So—a triphammer is—is the natural sound of a man-made machine that isn't there."

It seems to make her happy. Makes her see "Triphammer" in a new light. Not a trigger part. I turn out the little brass lamp on my desk. We kind of half sit and half lie down here on the carpet in the reddish glow of my heater.

Judy Cook and I go way back, fifteen years anyway. At times she has been my closest friend. On other occasions, my sworn enemy. Judy is tall, five ten, skinny as a beanpole. To describe her physically would depend on what era you were talking about, because her hair and her glasses have gone through a dozen combinations. When first we were close, she had her hair dyed red and kind of up in a bun, bat-lady glasses with frames all gold with rhinestones or whatever. Then her hair was silver for a while, and she wore contact lenses, which made her eyes all red. Then she let her hair come out naturally gray, and she had oversize square glasses, the lenses tinted all smokey blue, like she was skiing in Europe. Her makeup has gone from heavy to none at all. Judy's got a pleasant face with big teeth; hardly a beauty, she's spent her life being "a great gal." But she is extremely high-strung. Very vulnerable, sensitive to the smallest slight. You often find her desk empty, and she's back in the restroom having a little cry. I myself have offended her by some little remark I wasn't even aware of. She's one of those people who takes things way too much to heart. Very little control over her feelings. Her life is constantly jumping. Every couple of years she tenders her resignation, on some matter of principle, and the chief always talks her out of it.

We got to be friends when we were both on the rebound from broken marriages. Sheila had left me for good—moved to Buffalo and taken Dickie with her. That was when my drinking went completely out of control. Long winter nights alone. My whole world had fallen in on me. I didn't care about anything. My dependence on alcohol got so bad I couldn't straighten up and fly right when Dickie would come to visit. One Thanksgiving I didn't even make it to Sunday. I felt this cold fog enveloping me Saturday night as I crossed the wet pavement to the liquor store. Sunday morning I was not hung over, I was still drinking. I had to call Judy Cook to drive us to the bus station. I never before had felt so defeated as I did lying down in the backseat listening to Judy and Dickie having a merry little conversation. I was in terrible shape all through that time. Almost lost my job. The chief read me the riot act: "Pull yourself together, Triphammer, or you're gone."

Judy probably had it even worse. Without warning one day her husband just walked out the door and never looked back. Leaving her with two teenage boys and no child support. I often think I have terrible troubles, and then I see people face adversities far worse and do heroic things I doubt I would ever be able to do. Judy put one boy through college, the other one went into the Marine Corps. Judy kept things together, working all sorts of extra jobs that left her bleary eyed. I don't know how she did it. Somehow she muddled through. Without her help I don't know how I could have made it with Dickie the first couple of years. Judy was like a mother to him. Actually, she was like a mother to me, too. She never complained about my drinking; she'd sit up far into the

night while I blubbered away feeling sorry for myself.
Often she'd spend the night. Lie there in the dark and eat
one of Dickie's Hershey bars while I snored so loud it
rattled the windows. Judy never asked for anything in
return. Made a lot of delicious dinners for us, at our
house and at hers. We spent Christmases together, when
her two boys would come home. Their father would call
and have to ask which one he was speaking to.

I cannot say, truly, I didn't see what was going on. I
saw. I just chose not to deal with it. For some reason,
Judy Cook fell in love with me. We were both very
vulnerable, both having been recently deserted. As I say,
I am sure she fell for me on the rebound from her
worthless husband. She has two acres of lawn out at her
house in the country, and I'd always mow it for her. I'd
do all sorts of jobs around the house, Mr. Fix-It. It was
nice—we went places together, like to restaurants and a
show, and I was very dependent on her, so far as my
home life with Dickie went. But I never thought of her
that way. And then one day I happened to find out that
she had told her "rap group" that she and I were lovers. I
brooded about it. Finally I mentioned it to her, out at her
house, sitting in front of the fire after she had made me
this beautiful dinner. At first she denied it. She said,
"Trip, when we sleep together, we *sleep* together!" But
eventually she did say that the other women might have
got the impression we were lovers, and she did not correct
them. She got all red and upset. She said in this angry
little whisper, "You won't lose respect in this community
if people think you sleep with me."

I said, "I'm not exactly worried about my reputa-
tion." And I wasn't. Of course not. But I felt funny. It

always upsets you when you fail to reciprocate strong feelings like that. It puts you in a bind.

We sat there watching the fire die out. Hell hath no fury, I said to myself. And felt ashamed. I didn't know which way to turn. She had always been so gentle and steadfast. She would always drop whatever she was doing and come help me if I was in trouble. I had opened my heart to her and told her things I never even told my wife.

Dickie had a little part in the seventh grade play, and I took Judy to opening night. When Judy and I showed up, there were Patsy and Kitty saving seats for us. Judy fumed all through the evening, she wouldn't even stand in the hall with us during intermission. Rude as shit to Patsy. And at the end, when we came back to my house for coffee, Judy pulled herself up and said, "Now your girlfriend's got me mad!" That's when she started this thing about how I only love women for their bodies, they're my playthings.

I didn't help things. I'd bad-mouth Patsy to her, especially when the trouble with Kitty got going. Judy would say, "But you sleep with Patsy." And I'd get all red in the face. "Admit it," Judy would say, "Patsy is a selfish and incompetent mother, you have no respect for her, but still you sleep with her. Because at forty years of age, you are hot for her bod."

Then Patsy and I finally called it quits. I lost Patsy. I lost Kitty. There was this big void in my life. And once again Judy Cook filled it up. We got back on our former footing. Except, without a word said, we had new ground rules. Didn't open up as much, didn't talk about forbidden subjects. It was a bit superficial. But it passed the time. Friendly, easy, a bite to eat and a movie. She didn't stay over at my house; we'd say good-bye at eleven o'clock. It wasn't exactly fulfilling, but at least things didn't blow up in your face all the time.

And then they did. I didn't sleep with a woman for months after Patsy. I had put so much of myself into her and all the turmoil with poor Kitty that I just felt drained. Didn't want to get involved with anyone. Needed time to heal up. The problem is that I did. The old sexual drive came back. I was itchy as hell. I was keeping my eye out all the time. I didn't want anything very serious, just something physical and fast. Didn't want love. Wanted to get laid. And the opportunity presented itself one afternoon when I was checking out a complaint about an intruder. Some lost soul walked into a big house and warmed his tootsies at the dying fire. The lady of the house came downstairs and found him asleep there, a bum, a homeless old fart. I had to go down and speed him on his way. The lady took a liking to me. After I deposited the bum at the bus station with a one-way ticket and a ham sandwich, I went back to the house.

I should have known better. She was married, her husband was a high mucky-muck in the finance office at the college. Head full of figures all day, he did not tend to his husbandly duties. This very attractive woman going to waste. She was so hungry for it you could almost hear her loneliness, like a high-pitched siren. You could see the desperation in her eyes. I was quite soft-spoken and noncommittal. But I got the message across to her, what she had on her mind was perfectly all right with me. She had a boy in junior high, like I did, and we made up this bullshit pretense to have a talk about the lads. She said she'd bring lunch over to my house.

And she did, this big elaborate affair, a seafood quiche. I had spiffed up in clothes easy to get out of, and she was in costume, with all these bracelets and rings and necklaces and perfume and makeup. We wasted no time—we embraced and kissed right in the kitchen while she was heating up the quiche. She had brought along a joint of marijuana and was disappointed when I did not join her, but we ran right through a big bottle of cold Chablis. I went into the kitchen and took the phone off the hook. She smoked half the joint before lunch and the other half with the home-baked apple pie. She laughed, she said the dope made her a bit paranoid. All the while I am smacking my lips over the delicious food and wondering what is awaiting me beneath her gypsy costume.

At the table we hold each other's hands and look into each other's eyes. She bad-mouths her husband, says he doesn't understand her, he's always away on trips and takes little interest in his family. A workaholic. And her life is pretty disappointing to her, endless rounds of boring dinner parties. Her bracelets clang. I'm biding my time. I have only one thing on my mind, and I see there is no possibility for any long-term thing here. I don't even like her that much. I'm a little ashamed of myself. Taking advantage of this woman's unhappiness with her lackluster life. I want her to quit her sob story and get to it. But I sit here and listen, thinking it will be worth it in a moment or two.

She prattles on, and eventually I have to take matters into my own hands. I rise. I walk around the table. I lean down over her, and she looks up at me. Her eyes say, "Let us commit adultery, let us sin." I have a quick thought of backing out—this woman might be a lot of problems.

I think of her poor husband over there buried in his ledgers, not suspecting for a moment that the constable on patrol, whose salary he pays with his taxes, is violating his happy home. His unhappy home. I say in my slightly woozy Chablised head that this is no time for scruples. I lift her up and we stand here, and she is shaking all over with lust and fear. I pull up her long dress and get my hands around the globes of her rather boyish ass, and that is when I look over her shoulder out my front window and see Judy Cook's old Dodge Dart pull into the driveway behind my paramour's Volvo. I straighten immediately and pull away.

"Oh," I say, "I seem to have company."

My newfound lady friend panics and goes into the kitchen to hide. I go out the front door to head Judy off. She is gazing at the Volvo. She has some papers for me from the chief; she says she tried to call me but the line was busy. I take the papers and do not invite her in. She has this rather dazed expression. I guess she smells the wine on my breath. As I walk her to her car, she is silent for a while, and then she says, motioning to the Volvo, "Is it Patsy?"

I say kind of angrily, "No, it's not Patsy." I am sensitive to Judy's moods. I can tell how much trouble she is having with it.

She says, "C'mon, it's Patsy."

I deny it again. I'm very confused, a boy with his hand in the cookie jar. I open her car door. I say, "I have matters to attend to."

She says, "I'll bet you do."

I go back inside and find my gypsy queen sitting on the black stool by the phone, trembling like crazy. I nuzzle her for a minute or two. I take her hand, and I intend to lead her right by the table down the hall to my room where I have fresh sheets on my bed. But we don't make it by the table. She lets out a little gasp and I follow her panicky eyes and I see that Judy is still out there sitting in her car. My lady friend goes back to the kitchen to the black stool. I stand in the dining room all distraught. I wait. I wait and wait. Finally Judy gets out of the car and comes to the door.

She says, "I can't get my car started."

I say, "I will start it for you."

She says, "No, I have to call the Triple A."

I think, Swell, oh, swell. There is a rustle in the kitchen like a big dog has got loose. Then I hear the creak of the basement door.

I say to Judy, "Please sit in my living room. I'll call the Triple A." Judy would be in the kitchen if I were not blocking her way. I am extremely angry. I am also sad. It's like Judy is helpless now. She's got to see who it is. She stares at the debris on the table. She smells the pot in the air. And the perfume. I notice the big black leather handbag on the floor.

I say to Judy, kind of fast, taking her arm, "You just sit in the living room until the Triple A—"

To my utter astonishment Judy violently pushes my hand off her arm. She goes to the front door. It's started to rain, and she just stalks out into it. She gets into the middle of my front yard, and then she turns around and yells like to wake up the dead, "You son of a bitch!"

I step out onto the porch and say, "You're welcome to wait until the truck comes."

That infuriates her. She walks out to the curb and

then turns around again and screams, "You fucker—you *fucker!*" Then she runs off down the street in the rain.

I watch her go. I know she is not a pushy woman. Not a superficial one. I know she feels humiliated. Using language like that, at the top of her voice. She is always so soft-spoken, kind of polite and dainty in her speech. For her to scream at me like that means she's blown all her fuses. I watch her hotfoot it around the corner. I do not feel pity for her. I feel very much stronger and deeper emotions.

But I have this problem. I go back inside, and the kitchen's empty. I go down into the basement. There's Gypsy, standing in front of the washer-dryer, shaking like a leaf. I look into her eyes and I think the Russians have landed. Clearly, our sexual appointment has been canceled. She says she has to go home, she knew this was a mistake. I say, "No, no, there's no mistake. Calm down." But she brushes by me and goes upstairs and begins to gather her pots and pans and put them back into the brown grocery bags she brought them in. She looks out the window and emits a wail. She can't leave, Judy's Dodge is right behind her Volvo. I say please stay, everything's going to calm down in a minute. But the whole thing is too much for her reefer-riddled brain to deal with. I go out, and luckily Judy did not take her car keys with her, and the Dodge starts right up. I pull it out and park it on my front lawn. That done, I hop out and try to persuade my new friend to stick around. But she is busy with her packages, dumping them in the Volvo. She gets behind the wheel, and I say, "Please call me," and she says, "Ha!" She backs out right into my mailbox, knocks it flat, and then roars away.

I stand here in the rain.

I go inside and pour myself a big slug of Scotch and sip it slowly in my black Barcalounger.

In half an hour I hear a car start out there. It's Judy. She squeals away in her Dodge. I do nothing.

I'm still sitting in my chair when Dick comes home from school. I'm half in the bag. He asks what happened to our mailbox. I say it grew weary of this life. I tell him the whole goddamn story. He is nervously eyeing my drink. My tongue is loose. I go into all the grim details. A smile flickers on his face. He asks questions. By the time I am finished, he thinks it is all very funny. Though he is worried about poor Judy. Only then do I come to my senses and realize I should not have told him.

Come to think of it, that's when I took the little green book Judy gave me for my birthday and put it down in the basement by the old fish tank. I probably would have burned the book had I known the full extent of what she had done. Later I discovered that she took down the Volvo license plate number and ran a data on the teletype at the station. I had visions of her anonymously calling the husband over at the college and saying, "It's noon, do you know where your wife is?"

So for a few months Judy Cook and I are on the outs again. I lose track of her affairs and she loses track of mine. We are overly polite at the office. I have learned my lesson and do not misbehave. I go into permanent celibacy. I make one halfhearted attempt with a new girl at the bank, but she tells me how her life turned completely around when she gave it to Jesus.

Then, sure enough, eventually Judy and I have a little supper at the Antlers and our weird relationship is

off and running again. Which is when the all-time worst
thing happens. This one is serious.

I drank heavily that night, I guess I got pretty ram-
bunctious. I remember making out with her on the
couch. French kissing. Feeling her breast. I don't know
quite what happened after that. But in the morning, my
head pounding, I fixed Dick his breakfast and got him off
to school, and then Judy came out of my room and sat
down at the dining room table with me. She had this
huge black eye.

I was taken completely by surprise. I said, "Jesus,
where'd you get that shiner?"

She just looked daggers at me. She said she had a
splitting headache. She said she was going to skip work.

I said, "Did you bump into something?"

But all she would give me was the silent treatment.
She went home. I called her during the day and got no
answer. And then about five o'clock her Dart pulls into
the driveway, and she gets out and comes into the house.
In the intervening hours the shiner has developed. Now
it's this huge purple discoloration that goes down her
cheek and also disappears up into her hair. She looks like
she's been whacked with a board. She sits there, clearly
in pain, and she says, "I just want you to look at it. I want
you to see what you did!"

I cannot believe it. I say, "I've never hit a woman in
my life. Even when it got bad with Sheila, I never raised
a hand to her. I have no respect for a man who would hit
a woman. I never hit Patsy."

Judy says, "Of course not, she's high-spirited, and
she might hit you back."

I hear it, and I cringe. I turn away. Her face is a

wreck. I do not believe I got drunk enough to do that. And not remember. I do remember making out on the couch.

Judy sighs. She says Jeremy, her older boy, the marine, is home visiting. He wants the name of who did this to his mother. She says she won't tell him. She just had to come over and let me take a good look. And then she loses it. She cries. I can't hardly bear to see those tears flowing down that horrible puffy and discolored cheek. Before she gathers herself up and wanders in a daze back out to her car, she says something that makes me extremely ashamed. She says, "And you were the only man I ever felt safe with!"

The next few days are a nightmare. I replay the whole evening over and over in my mind. I have absolutely no memory of it. Apparently my drinking has gotten so far out of control that I am experiencing blackouts. Never before have I become violent or abusive. I always just get sodden. When Judy comes back to work, she's wearing dark glasses. She looks so terrible that the other officers don't even make the usual little cracks, like "Did you run into a door, ha-ha?" She says she fell on the ice. I can hardly bear to be in the office. I resolve never to drink again. I am sick to my stomach. I take her aside. I wish she'd see a doctor, she might have a concussion.

That weekend she calls me and asks can she come over. I say of course. She does come over. She says, "I never said you actually hit me." She clings to her pride; she says that she always called it "what I had done." I do not remind her that she said Patsy would "hit back." *Hit* back. She may not even remember saying that part. But clearly she has decided I have suffered enough, and now she is setting the record straight. We sit at the dining room table, across from each other. She pretends she is just going over the story again the way she always told it. But we both know she led me to believe something else and did not correct me. But now she says, "We were in your den, and you were too drunk to walk down the hall and get into bed. I tried to help you. And you fell."

I remember falling. I lost my balance and went crashing to the floor. I banged up my shoulder.

She says calmly, "You bumped into me. I lost my balance and went face-first into the wall."

I am so relieved.

Then after she was gone, I thought about it. And I got very sick at heart. It certainly matters, to me anyway, that I didn't hit her. But she was only trying to help me, and she got that awful blow to the face. I was DWI, in my own home. Drunk drivers don't remember they ran over a child. They didn't *mean* to. They just take out their personal problems on the public, no self-control, get into such a state they have no regard for the rights of others. That's how I was in my den. After making out with her and holding her breast. But she wanted me to do it sober, because I cared for her. She was devoted to me. Only man she ever felt safe with.

They call it a residence hotel, but the Palermo is really just a flophouse. It's a place where transients and down-and-outers can hang their hats. Not a crack house, like in big cities, but pretty drug infested. Winos and bums. I hate to get a call from the Palermo because I know that one way or another it will be nasty. And in early March, when I am on graveyard, I get this call at 4:00 A.M. that two men are arguing violently in an upstairs apartment at the Palermo.

More and more, as the years go by, I dislike this part of the job. I just can't get my heart into it the way I used to do when I was young and full of piss and vinegar. By the time I get there, they have moved it out into the hallway. Both of them six-footers, two hundred pounds, one considerably older than the other. And both sporting facial cuts. I try to separate them—they are swearing and cussing and bouncing around in the hallway. They wrestle with me, especially the older subject. I have to resort to my nightstick, and I whack him on the collarbone. But he is very drunk and not too responsive. I thwack him a second time, across the back. But he grabs my windpipe and chokes me half to death. I can't hardly slow him down. I hit him in the kneecaps and the elbows, I hit him on the shoulder. Two or three times I hit him in the face, I hit him in the side of the ear with my fist. I've done enough to lay out three men and his only response is to get more perturbed. We got blood everywhere, his ear is flowing, and I'm not sure that he doesn't have a tooth out. His wounds bleed pretty good. Finally I get him cuffed. The younger fellow is fairly subdued, lying on the couch back in the apartment. Neither man seems to know why they have been fighting. The apartment is trashed, blood on the walls, windows broken, holes in the sheetrock. I finally get the young man to explain. These boys are father and son. It has been a family quarrel, a dispute over money. They sit talking to each other, both cuffed, and the father spits at his kid and kicks him. They are calling each other all sorts of names; they are not too happy with each other.

I charge them both. I get them in the cuffs back to the office and start to process them. I take the cuffs off the father, and as soon as they are off, he takes a swing at me, clips me hard. So I backhand him. I tackle him and get him down on the floor. I decide to hell with printing him or photographing him, I won't uncuff him again until after he's arraigned. I call the judge. The judge comes down, the way he always does, all dressed up in his blue suit and red bow tie, wearing his bedroom slippers. The father swears at the judge, he rants and raves pretty incoherently, screaming, "You fucker, you mother-fucking bastard!" The judge calmly decides that the best place for him is jail. The son is halfway rational, so the judge lets him off with instructions to appear the following Tuesday, court night. The father, however, is to be committed. The son does not seem too agitated by it. I take the father to the county jail, to a holding cell. As soon as I uncuff him, we got the same deal, so I push the electric button and pop him in. He beats his head against the bars. Every time he does it, he splits the skin. Then he tears the sink off the wall, breaks that, throws it into the toilet, breaks that, and pieces of white porcelain fly all over the inside of the cell. He's barefoot, so he gets his feet all cut to shit. I need some assistance from the deputy, and we go in and handcuff this bastard, hands and feet both. We throw him on a cot. The man's got more problems than just booze. He doesn't even seem to know he's hurt, so now I got to take him up to the emergency room and have him checked out for injuries, and document that in my report to make sure it is clear that he did it to himself. He is one fucking mess, lacerations all over the place. They give him a tranquilizer shot that straightens him out right away.

I'm getting too old for this. In my twenties I could handle it. Even well into my thirties. But now I'm just not capable. I'm an animal well past its prime, no longer hungry for the kill. Maybe I should put in for crossing guard at an elementary school. I am all-over cuts and bruises. It's a wonder I didn't go into cardiac arrest just from hitting him so hard. I am in a very sorry state back in the office, just sitting there at seven-thirty, slumped over a cup of coffee. What I need, of course, is my Scotch. I sit looking forward to my den and the all-over warm feeling of the alcohol running through me.

But what reward do I get for my labors? When the chief comes in at quarter to eight, he is extremely hot under the collar. Right when he calls me into his office, I can see how steamed he is. He throws the morning paper across the desk at me and says, "Would you like to explain that big photograph on page one?"

I have no idea what this is about. I spread the newspaper before me and stare at a photograph of the demonstration march over at the college yesterday. There I am in my uniform, big as life, walking along with Sydney. She never passes up a march, and a half hour before this one she called me all in a panic and asked me if I would be a darling and bring over her VCR tape of *Sunset Boulevard*. I said, "Sure, absentminded professor." And I did walk around the circle with her. But we were just planning dinner. I explain this to the chief.

The chief says, "You got no lady friend, Triphammer." He says it like I couldn't have one.

That gets me steamed up. I say, "Well, I certainly do."

He says, "You never brought anybody to the Christmas party."

I am getting agitated to a considerable degree, resenting this intrusion on my private life.

The chief says, "Even if what you say is true, why didn't you just take her out of the line?"

I have no answer for that. Except to say it never crossed my mind.

The chief says, "We do not put the uniform on display in a union dispute. No matter what your lady friend urges you to do." He sits forward and folds his hands on his desk. "That's all for now, Trip. You look a bit worse for wear this morning. Go home and take off your shoes."

I'm so mad that when I get home, I drink angry. Always a mistake to drink angry. I get a little emotional, thinking up ways to get back at the chief. Some of my plans are pretty elaborate. I wish I had been marching with the workers, so long as I'm going to get blamed for it. I'm as mad as a wet hen. I visualize the chief taking a second look at the newspaper photograph and thinking to himself that I am robbing the cradle. I am fit to be tied.

I think back to when he first took over the reins as chief. His predecessor, Bartoli, had put little demerits and negative things in my personnel file, like lack of ticket production. I figure Bartoli was just doing that to have something on me if he'd ever need it. But I didn't like it; it put a little shaded area on my career. And then our new chief goes to the Public Safety Committee, three members of the board, not the full board, and he brought up these blemishes on my record. He never consulted with me as to whether the charges were true. Lo and behold, prior to our raises coming out in June our new chief called me into his office and gave me this public relations crap about working together, and taking the bull by the horns, which was his favorite expression back then—he was always taking the bull by the horns. He told me he was withholding my pay raise. It was only about five hundred bucks, but it was a big deal to me. What with all my then-wife's expenses, I needed every penny. Besides, it irritated the shit out of me because I was in effect being told that I was not a suitable employee performing at an efficient pace. I wanted to tell him to stick it in his ass. I contemplated doing lots of small things to annoy him. But then I figured that that would just prove his point, that I didn't take the bull by the horns.

I acted like nothing had happened. But I hired an attorney whose house I had painted that summer, and he said the thing wasn't legal. We discussed the matter at length in his office. He wrote a letter to the board saying it was against civil service regulations to withhold a person's pay without prior notice as to just cause. The chief wouldn't budge. But he checked with the city attorney and was told it was not legal. So he asked me to come in and talk with him. I did. I took a tape recorder. It was my little way of letting him see I was taking the bull by the horns. My attorney told me just not to sign anything. By now the relationship between the chief and me was barely civil at best, all nit-picky. We both knew he was just flexing his muscles. The other officers were behind me because they could see that if this new guy beat me down, then their asses could be next in line. Things dragged on. My attorney finally filed a petition in court. So the mayor himself got hold of me. I was on lunch break, and the mayor talked to me while I sat there eating my sandwich. He said the board would reconsider. He didn't say they were wrong. He said the chief had reported that my work had improved, and I was producing more tickets, which was a lie. I hadn't changed a thing I did. They just wanted to back down. But I would not let them off the hook. Finally they had to reinstate my raise. I had proved the chief could not ride roughshod over the men. It is not forgotten. I still think about it.

Actually, the chief is often foolish. One day last September I got a call that there was a fire at the old A & P. I whipped over, and it was a fire, a small one set off by a welder's torch. I put it out with CO_2. I canceled the firetrucks which were heading that way, two engines

and a ladder truck. But in the meantime the chief pulls
in; he had heard it on his radio. He got out and ran over
to my car, and he sees the A & P has been turned into
this huge pile of rubble. He had just got back from a
month's vacation, and he was not aware of the fact that
the building was in a state of demolition. He gets on my
radio and says, "Jesus, don't cancel those trucks, send all
the fire and rescue units you got, we have a major explo-
sion on our hands here, big heaps of rubble, tons of stone
and iron."

I tried to shut him up, but he kept jabbering away to
the dispatcher about tons of stone and iron. Finally I say,
"But, Chief, they are demolishing this building to make
way for a parking ramp."

Take the bull by the horns, tons of stone and iron.

For some reason it defuses my anger. Thinking of
the chief's stupidity. Every police person will do something stupid now and then. Last week, around 3:30 A.M.,
a bunch of us were having coffee down at the diner on
Route 13, two or three sheriff's cars, me, Vandermark,
and a trooper car with Linda, the female trooper. We were
just shooting the shit, busting each other's chops. Linda
has a hell of an arm on her, she teaches self-defense at
the academy. And she was bitching about having to wear
her vest. It's hard enough on a guy, but she was pissing
and moaning about how "one size fits all" doesn't work
so hot on a woman, how she hates the way it looks under
the pleats of her shirt. She says it sticks your boobs out
like shoehorns. She goes off to get back on the road, and
then the rest of us do. I had to go back to the office and
pick up my teletypes. On the way up I see a car on the
median, halfway up the long hill of Route 13. When I get

closer, I see it's Linda in her trooper car. I think she's
parked there to run the radar. But then I see she's tearing
the shit out of the tires, the front bumper and the back
bumper are jammed up on opposite sides of the culvert,
she's stuck in there. Apparently she had to cut across the
median to nail a violator speeding down the hill in the
southbound lanes. So all of us guys pull our cars onto the
grass, like we are going to give her a hand. Instead,
however, we circle our cars around her and turn our
spotlights on her. We really light her up. She gets out
cussing, madder than a bastard. But now she's one of the
guys. You got to do something stupid to be one of the
guys.

So I think about that. All sorts of things. I am sitting
here drowning my anger at the chief. I hurt all over my
body from those two Palermo bastards. The booze is a
sedative for my emotional and physical pains. But then
Sydney shows up. She walks in and finds me. She is pretty
appalled to see what I have gotten myself into. The sad
look in her eyes slows me down to a crawl. We sit in my
den and share a salad. She sips at a Coke, and I try to pull
out with a beer. Previously she has let my little episodes
go by without comment. This time she takes a stand.
She says, "I'm concerned about your drinking."

I find her attitude a bit annoying. She is adopting
this superior tone with me. I feel like a naughty boy who
has to stay after school. I get all stupid and defensive. I
say something I would not have said if I were sober. To be
honest, I probably would have thought it, I just wouldn't
have said it. Booze turns off the warning bell. I say, "Well,
you're Jewish."

This pricks up her ears.

I say, "I read an article somewhere about how Jews have an extremely low rate of alcoholism. As an ethnic group. Compared to the Irish, who seem to be the worst offenders. Swedes get into it pretty good. But Jewish people don't seem to have a taste for it. No tradition of getting blitzed. You know, like an Irish wake."

She's still looking at me funny.

I say, "Of course, there is another school of thought. Some people say all you have to do—to understand why there are so few Jewish alcoholics—is taste a glass of Manischewitz."

She is not too amused.

I say, Jesus, don't look at me that way. All I mean is I grew up with it. My stepfather liked his whiskey on Saturday night. In my younger days smokin' and drinkin' was a sign of manhood. You weren't even born yet, you don't understand the fifties. Getting drunk was a natural thing. It was funny. It wasn't a "problem." We had little respect for the few individuals who made it a constant thing and neglected their jobs and their families. But it was quite acceptable to tie one on now and then. Clean out the pipes. I say, "You don't understand."

"Because," she says, "I am a Jew?"

"Oh, you know I didn't mean that."

We sit here. Me and my big mouth. I apologize for speaking out of turn. I ask her if she has ever been discriminated against. I thought that sort of thing was pretty much in the past. I say, "Have you ever been on the receiving end of it?"

"Sure."

She tells me this ugly little story. For one year, seventh grade, she went to private school. "There were only about three Jews in my grade," she says. "And this little guy, Martin Speno, he'd come to my locker every day and call me 'Jew Dog.' "

" 'Jew Dog'?"

"That's right."

"Doesn't sound right to me. 'Jew Dog' is what you'd say to a *guy*. Like in a sword fight—'Put up thy weapon, Jew Dog.' Wouldn't you call a girl a 'Jew Bitch'?"

She shakes her head and mutters something ironical which I don't quite catch. Then she says, "I dreaded going to my locker. Martin Speno got other boys to do it. Even one guy who had said he liked me and thought I was pretty."

I visualize her as a seventh grader. I don't know why I see her skinny, but I do, I see her at the height she is now. But she hasn't filled out, no boobs or anything. I see her cringing by her locker, with this little semicircle of boys around her. We've never talked about this subject before. Sitting here in my den she seems different, far away. I ask her, "Why didn't you report it to the principal?"

She says, "I never told anybody. Not even my parents."

"But they should know. They'd pull you out of that private school right quick."

She just sits here kind of sad. She's thoughtful. She says, "It took me completely by surprise. I didn't know how to deal with it. And it went on for weeks. That's why I didn't tell my parents. I was ashamed to tell my father that I had let it happen to me. I felt I'd have to explain why I just took it."

She looks pretty forlorn. She says, "They say you are

not supposed to talk to a person about their drinking problem while they are drinking."

"I'm not drunk. I can hear you."

She waits a minute, looking at me, and then she says, "They don't make them like you anymore."

It's kind of a double-edged remark. Or so I take it. I feel honored and cast aside at the same time. Like a noble relic.

She says, "You have values. You take them seriously, and you try to live by them. Do you know how few people do that?"

I am embarrassed.

"And," she says, "drinking doesn't go with that. The way you get, Trip, when you drink—"

I interrupt her. I say, "I don't get so bad. Not all loud and belligerent." In the back of my mind, however, is the time I fell on Judy Cook.

She says, "You're kidding yourself. How can you not notice?"

"How can I not notice?"

"Dick," she says. "Dick hates it. You know that. You're a devoted father. But how can he take advantage of your love? Every time you drink you push him away from you."

She comes and sits down beside me on the floor. She puts her hand up on my leg. She says, "You know that if you weren't drinking we'd be in bed right now."

This is true. I'm ashamed to look at her.

"You would never drink on your job. Dick and I are your job, too. We feel cast out when you do this."

Well, shit.

"I can't live with it. You can say it's because I'm Jewish—"

Oh, for Christ's sake.

She says, "I carry it with me all the time. In the middle of something I'll find myself thinking, Is he doing it now? Will he be that way tonight? You don't get points for not turning into Mr. Hyde. I hate the way you get all heavy. I hate the smell of it—"

She pulls away from me, sits back on the carpet like she finds the odor offensive right now. "And," she says, "I don't like the way you touch me. When you drink, your hands are different—"

Enough.

"You remember when you told me the most beautiful part of my body?"

I look into her eyes.

"C'mere," she says. She stands up and holds out her hand. I stumble up, and she leads me into the bathroom and makes me face myself in the mirror. Many is the time I have looked at myself in this mirror, and chuckled, and talked to myself, and winked, the way drunks will. But now I have to face it. My eyes are puffy, and I cannot escape what they tell me. I am trapped.

I realize I am not being bawled out. I am not being kept after school as a lesson to me. I look into her eyes in the mirror. She is asking me something from very deep in her heart.

There are probably vast numbers of people who have terrible sex lives, but they don't know it, so who cares? If you got nothing to compare it to, you can just think you're at the top of the heap and have the best deal in town. Trouble is, I do have something to compare it to. Always before, when I reached the high point of the party, I felt like my dick didn't belong to me: *I* was attached to *it*. *It* was the brains in the family. It had a life of its own. Now I'm not near as powerful. It is very depressing. I read this article in the newspaper about a horrible condition brought on by years of alcohol abuse, "testicular atrophy." It is especially prevalent in bourbon drinkers, which, thank God, I am not. In advanced stages it can lead to loss of facial hair and complete impotence. Your balls shrink to pea size. I get very nervous and inspect my nuts, and can't decide whether they've gotten smaller. I worry, though, that my penis no longer emerges like a missile from a silo, there's this kind of reluctance to it. Which is a shame, given I am falling so totally in love with Sydney. If we don't panic and rush matters, if we take as long as possible, it is still the loveliest experience life has to offer. And we do it every which way. She says things are fine with her. But she is such a kind soul she'd say that. I think my problem is that there's no traffic cop down there—when the blood rushes to "engorge," it has no sense at all and engorges everything in the area. I get completely confused, dying to fuck and dying of pain. Like what Thomas Jefferson said about having a wolf by the ears, you don't know whether to hold on or let go.

We stake out my rear end as our number-one priority. Fix that, and maybe these other symptoms will disappear. I go to Syracuse to a specialist. He examines me and tells me I got "a third-degree prolapse of the mucosal membrane." Which in plain language means the lining of my butt is falling out. This is why I can't play Ping-Pong with Dick in the basement anymore. This is why I have such trouble getting in and out of cars. And this may be what is causing me to proceed under the yellow flag in bed. Dr. Mau, my specialist, is rather abrupt, like most doctors. They are really a terrible class of person—what with nurses and everybody kowtowing to them, they think they are God almighty. But I am so tired of being a drag I decide to have the first surgery of my life.

We schedule me to go up to Syracuse on the afternoon of March 17, and they'll cut and slash and tear me apart at eight the next morning. I check my benefits package, Blue Cross and Blue Shield, to make sure I'm covered. I got my maximum sick leave now, 960 hours. I flirt with the idea of claiming this as a job-related injury, all those years of walking a beat and sitting in a patrol car. We had a rookie once who claimed his neck was injured in the line of duty, a mere fender bender, and he collected benefits for thirteen years. He's a registered nurse and knows how to lead the bureaucrats astray with all the right answers. Collected his pay and all his raises over the years just like he was working. So I know you can fake it if you're smart enough. And I think maybe I can get away with it. You're involved in enough scuffles and scrapes and wrestling matches; guys are always getting hurt, especially bar fights or like my recent fracas at the Palermo. You get lots of injury time. But I am so embarrassed to be making elaborate plans for my rear end that I start lying about it right away. I tell the chief it's a hernia.

Sydney thinks I'm crazy to go up there all by myself. She wants to drive me and keep vigil. We argue about it for a week. Actually, I am scared to death that I won't be able to handle the pain. I do not want her to see me be a baby. I keep downplaying the seriousness of it. Dr. Mau says I ought to be able to come home in three or four days. I say that she will have plenty to do when I get home; she'll have on her hands a very impatient patient. Dick wishes me luck. He seems to think it's about as serious as a dental appointment.

So on the seventeenth I pack a little overnight bag and drive myself to Syracuse. They've told me I can have nothing orally after six, so I stop at a diner and load up with a big cheeseburger and a chocolate shake and a load of fries. At the hospital the admitting procedure only takes forever. They shuttle you from one office to another and take all your valuables away and lock them in the safe. I get X rays and urine tests and other assorted indignities. They put me in a double room way up on the sixth floor with a nice old gentleman who is recovering from a triple bypass. Various nurses come in and ask me all sorts of intimate questions. This one nurse gets all

freaked out about my blood tests. She says I've got a
blood sugar count of 460, over four times normal. I say I
wouldn't know about high blood sugar, must be my sweet
disposition. I pay for phone and TV. This very unpleasant
older nurse can't get her heart into my enema, especially
when I am already so tender down there and resist it. She
says I'm not trying, I'm not holding it. So she quits. I was
supposed to have two of them, but we hardly do one. I
use the phone, since I paid for it, and I have a nice long
talk with Sydney, who is staying with Dick in my absence. She says she may surprise me by showing up
tomorrow. I say, "Don't you dare." Dick comes on the
line for a moment and says after this I won't be such a
big asshole. I say heh-heh.

After a sleepless night, tossing and turning and
almost tearing the IV out of my arm, I am raring to go at
8:00 A.M. At nine. Ten. Eleven. I am itchy as hell. Not to
mention ravenously hungry. They don't come throw me
on a stretcher until two o'clock. Then I lie somewhere
down in the basement for another hour, and Dr. Mau
comes in with the blood of his last victim all over him.
He shakes my hand and says this won't take long. I'm
told I should not have a general anaesthetic. It usually
results in a longer recovery period, and it is especially ill-
advised for a person who smokes as much as I do. So I
think I am very wise and very brave when I consent to a
spinal. It's just a little sting, and before long I am dead
from the belly button down, can't feel a thing. They
wheel me in and roll me over onto this jointed operating
table. They lower the front, and all of me from my hips
to my head is a downward ski slope at a 45-degree angle.
They unhinge the rear and all of me from the base of my

bottom to my toes is another ski slope at 45 degrees the other way. My butt is sitting up top. They dig in. All I can feel is a kind of tugging. This really nice nurse keeps stroking my arms, and her husband is a cop too, so we chat about police work. I hear behind me everybody babbling away. No pain at all, I wonder why I ever worried. It doesn't even hurt in the recovery room, where I just lie in the bright light kind of stupid and not thinking clearly. Why did I waste so much time steeling myself? Back up in my room on the sixth floor I call home and tell Sydney the deed has been done. She surprises me. She cries.

I have a big dinner, veal parmigian. I watch TV. Then around midnight the spinal wears off. I move pretty quick from pain to agony to this unbearable state of things where I have a cannonball embedded in my ass. And the cannonball is in flames. I ring like a bastard for the nurses and get a big shot of Demerol, but it doesn't do a bit of good. The nurse says I'm not helping it along, it won't work if I don't give it a chance. I am determined not to be a baby, but these big sounds come out of me, moans and growls. I don't want to disturb my roommate, but I can't seem to swallow the sounds. I put my fist in my mouth and bite until the blood comes. I injure my head from swinging it frantically back and forth, hitting it against the bars. I struggle all through the night until four-thirty or five, and then I don't so much go to sleep as I just pass out.

By midmorning it eases off a bit. Dr. Mau comes in. He tells me the procedure was entirely successful. He says he had to remove more than anticipated, the total was about the size of a man's hand. I stare at mine. *A man's hand?*

Two days later I am bored to tears. I could kill for a cigarette. I convince Mau that I can do this recovery business just as well in the comfort of my own home. He says okay and signs me out. I persuade the nurse to give me one final big blast of Demerol for the voyage home. They're still worried about this blood sugar thing; they haven't once gotten it below three hundred.

I sit in my wheelchair in my room. It's Sunday. One thing that has eased my boredom is the NCAA basketball tournament. I watched two games on Saturday. Syracuse itself is in the thick of things, having been runner-up the year before. I'm sitting like a big gnome, my overnight bag clutched on my lap, when these giant black guys, with gold chains and about five pounds of jewelry each, come to wheel me downstairs. But we stay in the room staring at the TV. Syracuse is having a dickens of a time with this dark-horse sleeper team from Rhode Island. The black guys are on a first name basis with everybody on the Syracuse team. They watch the game with a far higher degree of sophistication than I do, and notice all sorts of things that I do not see at all. Syracuse loses. My bodyguards are out of sorts, and they don't take me down carefully. We wham into the elevator door and I jump a foot. When we get down to the lobby, we discover that on a Sunday afternoon the safe is closed. I can't get my valuables. The two black guys handle the problem by disappearing. Here I sit in my wheelchair.

Finally this big black woman nurse spies me and says, "What you doin' sittin' there all alone?" She raises heaven and earth, gets me my valuables, and then wheels me out, in a light snowfall, without her sweater, to 1 GROUCH in the parking lot.

She's freezing, and she says, "You aren't going to drive all by yourself?"

I say sure, and she helps me get my stuff into the car. She's so nice that suddenly I say, just like a black man, "Thankya, darlin'." I am afraid she'll be offended, but she gives me this big sunshine smile.

The first thing I do is stop at a little mom-and-pop's for a pack of cigarettes. I hobble in and come out and sit in the car and enjoy my first cigarette in days. It is outstanding. On the drive home in the snow flurries I realize that I am pretty goofy from the Demerol. I know that one of these things is my turn signal and the other's probably the gearshift. I am kind of chuckling to myself, going seventy. I am marveling at how smooth and relatively painless and quick this whole thing has been. Back in town I stop at our drugstore and get my codeine prescription filled.

Home sweet home. Nobody here. I pop some painkiller, lie on the couch, and doze. Dick's the first to show up, and we call Sydney, and my loved ones cannot believe how cheerful I am. Dick goes and gets a big load of Chinese take-out and we eat it in the living room and watch TV. Prone on the couch I wolf down a whole carton of fried rice. I'm real talkative. I describe my ordeal in minute detail, the way ladies who have had surgery do. I'm pretty smug. At bedtime Sydney fixes me a toasted cheese sandwich. She fusses around me a good bit before I drop into dreamland.

Three more days go by, kind of quiet and uneventful, before all hell breaks loose. Or doesn't. That's the prob-

lem. The uneasiness and discomfort in my gut builds
and builds. By dinnertime Sydney and Dick are pleading
with me to go to the hospital. My gut's jerking me around
so bad I actually fall off the bed. Dick wants to drive me
in his Chevy. Sydney wants to take me in her Honda. I
am in no condition to be behind the wheel of 1
GROUCH. Besides, I don't want no more hospital, I want
the comfort of my own home. By seven o'clock I am out
of my head with the cramps. Even the codeine fails to do
a lick of good. In the bathroom, drenched with sweat, I'm
knocked over by the pain again and almost shatter the
glass doors over the tub. We're all yelling. Before I know
she's done it, Sydney has put in the call, and an ambulance comes whipping into the driveway. Sydney and
Dick both want to go with me, but somehow in my
demented state I keep my wits about me and say that
means they'll be stuck up at the county hospital without
a car. One of them has to wait for a call and then bring
up whatever we forgot in our confusion. Their eyes look
at me all panicky, like the house is on fire. I blunder out
to the ambulance before the two young guys can bring in
the stretcher, and I throw myself in the back. Sydney
clambers in. She knows one of the young guys—he took
a film course from her at the college last year. While he's
checking all my vital signs and sticking this oxygen
mask in my face, he rattles on to her about *Stagecoach*. I
feel like I'm being cut in half. They got to give me some
relief, I can't stand it.

In the emergency room they do give me a shot of
something that stops my body from helplessly jumping
around. The doctor on call decides I have to be admitted.
He says I have an "impacted bowel." They stick an IV in

my arm and whip me upstairs to a private room, which looks pretty cozy to me as I mercifully go under.

They keep me a week. They say I'm all plugged up from everything I've eaten since my little feast in Syracuse the day before surgery. That goddamn Syracuse nurse didn't do her job—she only cleaned out the lower part and left all the food in the upper. And since then I've been eating like a horse. On the second day I ask the dietician what I did wrong. I want to avoid going through this again. She ticks off the most constipating foods you can eat. Topping the list are just what I took in, rice and cheese and chocolate. I couldn't have done a better job on myself had I tried. But the real culprit, she says, is the codeine. Which pills I have been popping like peanuts. So I got a week's worth of feasting in my midsection, and it's hardened like a big block of cement. They got to dig it out of me. And the only way to get to it is right through the new surgery.

We have three sessions a day, and each time they go up in there, I hit the ceiling. One nurse says I'm the worst case she's ever seen, even worse than the old people she has helped. Never have I felt so humiliated. It's an awful business.

But finally I feel better. Considerably weakened, though, and ashamed. I feel totally degraded. At least now I can appreciate Sydney's flowers. And she brings a get-well card from the office, signed by everybody. It's kind of a cute card with a goofy duck on the front wearing a pirate hat, and the words "Scuttlebutt has it . . . ," and you open it up to a picture of the duck walking the plank, and the words ". . . that your butt has been scuttled!"

I have been robbed of all my dignity. I have to wear

these giant diapers because I am incontinent. Sydney says people have been calling the house and want to come up and visit me. I say I am in no condition to receive well-wishers. I hate for anybody to see me like this. I hate for her to see it. The only nice part is Monday night when Dick and I watch the best basketball game we've ever seen, the NCAA finals—Kansas nips Oklahoma. I got so much dope in me I see the seams on the ball as it arcs toward the basket.

The nurses are tops. Only one sourpuss, all the rest are extremely kind. And really know their jobs. One especially, Phyllis, she kind of makes me her special pet. At first I didn't like her, she is so cheerful. But that's the way Phyllis really is; it's not an act. She does all sorts of nice things for me that she doesn't have to. Sits and talks with me at night, just to help me pass the time. She's short and chubby with a kind of boyish haircut. She's helped three AIDS victims die, right here in our little town. She says her husband is furious. He's sure she'll catch it and bring it home, with all the blood and fluids slopping around. But it's something she feels she must do. She feels about her job the way I feel about mine. I don't even mind it when she makes a mistake and calls Sydney my daughter. Phil blushes like a beet when I set her straight.

One thing that seems to worry everybody is this high-blood-sugar thing. It's still way up there in the four hundreds. They run some tests on me, and my liver's clean as a whistle, but they can't even find my pancreas. The booze seems to have eaten it. I don't produce any insulin at all. So they start giving me shots of it, and they tell me I am going to have to learn how to do it at home. Both my arms are dead from all the shots, but my real problem is I can't just stick the needle in *bang!* like they do. I got to worry it and start over in a new place. I do not enjoy letting Sydney in on the secret of what the years of drinking have done. She gets tears in her brown eyes as she watches me fuss with the needle, my hands shaking like crazy. Dick can't bear to watch it at all and turns away.

At odd hours I lie on my back and think this cannot be happening to me. Never in my life have I experienced anything remotely like it. I see I have misused the word "pain." I didn't know what I was talking about. And I see that even now I am still only sticking my toe in it. I'm in this private room because the hospital is overcrowded, and they've put me in the oncology ward. At night I hear what real pain is all about. Oldsters crying out in the darkness. This goes beyond pain, this is true suffering. One voice, every night, especially in the long hours before morning, doesn't even sound human. It's more like a big dog or some kind of animal, moaning and crying. Most terrible sound I ever heard. I ask an orderly if he can't give that man something. The orderly says that first of all it's a woman, and secondly they've already given her so much they're afraid of killing her. Which touches me very personally, especially when he says she'll never see the outside world again. They all know she is dying.

I had to face that with my own mother, there at the end. This makes me think of what she went through, and what I did about it and do not regret doing. I know she wanted me to do it for her. All shriveled up and horribly crippled from the arthritis. Stuck on that respirator, no possible cure. Half a dozen things wrong with her. The doctors wouldn't let her go. I pleaded with them. I said that they were not prolonging her life, they were prolonging her suffering. But they give you that crap about "once we start killing oldsters, where do we stop?" I suppose some of them are genuinely concerned, but I think a lot of them are just worried about getting sued by the family. When I could not get one glimmer of hope from a single doctor, I did it, and would expect Dick to do it for me if I ever get into such a state. You have to take things into your own hands in this stupid country where Death is a dirty word. Mom's eyes like hot coals in her little face. I knew what she was pleading with me to do. Although it is a very strange experience, since it is your mother who brings you into this world, the one who gives you the gift of life. And then you do this to her. I suppose that is what keeps most people from doing it. But it is the wrong way to think. Yourself is the wrong person to think about.

Which gets me to thinking about my mom. In the darkness, my brain all foggy with drugs, I see vivid little scenes way back in childhood. Like once my twin cousins, Gary and Glen, and I snitched one of our grand-father's cigars and climbed up into this mulberry tree at the back side of the house, a big tree. We were up there just even with the second-story windows. Big shots, passing around the cigar and swearing and telling dirty jokes. I happen to look over to the window and my mother's sitting there watching. She washed my mouth out with soap. Which was what a parent did back then. When we got that new '53 Hudson, she took me for a drive, and I kept egging her on to see what this swanky new car would do. Pretty soon we were doing eighty, the trees beside the road just flying by, and all of a sudden the state police were on our tail. We had to follow the trooper off the highway to the judge. Mom got fined thirty bucks. In 1953. Boy, the lecture she gave me. Both of us knowing it was really her own fault. She still talked about it years later, she never had any traffic infractions before that or since. I think of how I gave her so much trouble when I was in high school. A chronic truant. I had three junior years. I was twenty when I finally graduated. She was worried her Triphammer would never amount to a hill of beans. She got me a job at a gas station. Six to six. Eighty cents an hour. Not my cup of tea. They gave me every dirty job there was. I was a grease monkey. After three months I decided this was not the job for me, I was not going to spend my life doing this. So Mom let me quit if I'd go back to school. She was teaching me a lesson. I got good marks my senior year.

She was a tiny woman, just five foot. A hard little face. The oldest of seven kids. She only had an eighth-grade education. Went to work in an electric meter plant. Lived in a rented room, only went home on the weekends, to pay the coal bill. Her half sister, Amy, died in child-birth. Her mother died of cervical cancer soon after. So my mother raised the rest of the kids. Her first marriage, of which I am the sole product, was annulled after two months. I have never seen my real father. She called him a worthless drummer. I picture him tall, I sure didn't get my height from her. After me, when she was only nine-teen, she had a hysterectomy, a tumor removed. She was a very strict, stern mother. Lots of spankings. You make a scene in a store, you'd get your butt blistered, right there in the store. Or touch other people's things—she was a fanatic about touching other people's things. But if you didn't misbehave, she was very kind. I have no idea why I didn't listen to her about college. I could've gone. Avoid the fate of her and my stepfather. They were chicken farmers for a while. They built this big cinder-block building. One morning the water pipes broke in the night and all the chickens were frozen to the floor. So the folks gave that up. But what I remember most about my mother was her working from morning till night. She was always pitching in and slaving away at something.

It took me many years to discover that Mother was really a very tender person. She'd do anything in the world for people and not expect anything back. When Dad died, I realized how vulnerable she was. How dependent. When my stepfather went to his reward, having received none here below, it was like Mom was lost at sea in a little boat. Adrift. I could see it in her face. Like she had been abandoned. Nobody to guide the boat. After he was gone, she was very mopey. Her outlook had changed. Her personality was different. She was lonely. She had five or six operations and was in constant pain. She lost her sense of purpose. Didn't seem to have any drive. She'd dwell on things that didn't mean a tinker's damn. Always hated to ask people to do things for her. She'd never been scared of anything, or fearful, except of being alone. She didn't have that hair-trigger temper any more. Wasn't bullheaded like in her younger days. She'd seen too many people die. When she was young, her brother Dale died of diphtheria and her brother Edward of typhoid. Probably that is what made her reluctant to look on the bright side. She didn't smother you with syrupy emotions. Not getting constant approval from her taught me independence. Just do things. I realized you can get along in this world all by yourself if you have to.

Actually she was a very strong person. Never as a child did I see her cry. Never saw much affection between her and my stepfather. Come to think of it, she did get very low at funerals. And what could I do? Just try to be strong myself, hug her, and tell her things would be all right. From an early age I'd try to be strong for her. We went to a lot of funerals together. Her brother Lawrence died. Her brother Howard. Her sister's husband Anthony died. Each funeral seemed to take something from her that she would not get back. Tough lady, though. She weathered all the storms somehow. Except after my stepfather died. When I'd go over to comfort her, I'd work in his shop in the basement and keep expecting to see him come around the corner. She said it was like that for her. Around suppertime she'd expect him to come home to eat. But she always kept the lid on her deeper emotions. I was thinking of that just recently when Sydney and I were watching this old movie which Sydney was using in her course as an example of "proletarian realism," *The Grapes of Wrath*. But what made me light up was not the proletarian realism part, it was the mother. Right at the beginning, when her long-lost son comes home on parole from prison, she goes out in the yard to meet him. And she shakes his hand. Doesn't smother him with hugs and kisses. Shakes his hand. And at the very end of the movie I thought of Mom again when the mother in the movie says to her son that their family was "never of the kissing kind." That's my mom to a T.

A couple of years before she died, I did something smart. I bought us two tickets to Honolulu. I couldn't believe Dick didn't want to go. He was about eleven and all excited about this soccer camp up near Watertown. So it was just Mom and me for two weeks. On the big plane ride we were an hour late out of O'Hare and then another hour late out of LA. I was watching her like a hawk. She seemed very tired. Her age had slowed her down, and she didn't have the stamina she once had. We sat there together, and she was crocheting baby hats she makes for the nursery. She told me stories about a whole string of people long dead. But the closer we got to the Hawaiian islands, she began checking her watch every little while. She was excited and kept a sharp lookout. When we landed, she couldn't wait for the plane to come to a complete stop or for the other passengers to get out. In the taxi on the way to our hotel, she was all animated— look at this, look at that. She was just like a little kid. She could not believe how beautiful the Hawaiian islands were. All the varieties of flowers.

We had a room on the thirty-fourth floor of the hotel, with this view of the whole city, she'd sit out on the balcony and fall asleep looking at all the lights, just doze off in the warm breezes. She was already all crippled up, couldn't drive a car because she couldn't feel the gas or brake pedal with her feet. So I got her this wheel-chair—not really a wheelchair, a big wicker thing like for the boardwalk in Atlantic City. And I'd wheel her everywhere. We'd get to a place she wanted to be, and then she could take those few steps herself. Let her walk in stores. Flea markets. We went to the Hawaiian Hilton for the Don Ho show, which I thought was stupid but she found fantastic. Of course we had to go see where they filmed *Blue Hawaii* with Elvis Presley. And went out to the North Shore to see the thirty-footers. And the pine-apple fields. She couldn't take the bus tours. They had those straight-backed seats. We went to Pearl Harbor, to the Arizona Memorial. Her brother Howard, who by this time had died, was stationed in Pearl Harbor when it was bombed, and just missed being killed.

She bought herself a whole slew of Hawaiian printed dresses, and wore them all the time when we got home. Those two weeks just flew. She talked about it every day until she died.

It had been very sad for me to watch her year by year become less and less in charge. This woman who had worked all her life. I never let her go into a home. Others suggested it. But I saw my uncle in a nursing home, and it takes you from independence down to babyhood. Sitting there among people just waiting to die. So Mother stayed at home, watching her bird feeders, which I filled. She had a big thing about birds and could identify them all.

Once when I was still pretty little, I saw her do something at a funeral that really surprised me. She walked up to the casket and put her hand on the dead person's hand. It was what made me see that although she played this life very hard-nosed, she was an extremely tender person underneath it all. And at every funeral after that, I'd wait and watch for her to do it. She always did. It was her way of saying so long. To brothers, uncles and aunts, friends. It always struck me as strange, as I watched her do it over the years. It seemed to me that other people would do it, but they don't. Probably scared to touch a dead person. But Mom always reached in. Once when I was mad at her about something, I remember thinking, What you doing, Ma, seeking a pulse? She always did it, though. And that is why I did it with her when her time came. I reached in and put my hand on hers.

I buried my badge with her. I just slipped it into a crease in the satin. She was pretty proud when I made sergeant. Her life was no bed of roses. Not a happy life. Too many losses and disappointments. Too much work, work, work. I miss her every day and talk to her. Go to her grave on her birthday and tell her how Dick's doing. Discuss matters. I don't gloss things over or pretty them up. That would not be in keeping with who she was.

When they let me go home, I am still pretty much in pain all the time and do not at all feel like putting on a brave front for callers. But Sydney can't hold them off forever, and my first well-wisher is the chief. He seems to think it will cheer me up if he puts on a fashion show. So I just lie here all perspirey on the couch while he struts and prances in our new, spiffy, low-maintenance Dacron-and-wool-blend uniform. It's got gold-plated buttons that do not need burnishing—they don't even need buttoning. The reversible duty jacket has this space-age insulation with larger, higher-placed slits on both sides, to make it easier to get at your gun. It also has a police patch on each shoulder, which is good, because in the old uniform, if you happened to be facing the wrong way, a person wouldn't know whether you were a police officer or a private security guard or a postal employee. The pants have permanent creases, and the shoes are patent leather lookalikes that never need polishing. Four hundred seventy-six dollars. Chief is really tickled with it.

I let him make his own coffee. In my black Barcalounger he sits bent forward over his cup and tells me that the son of a dead officer has come in to the station. Chief says, "I just about shit. This twenty-one-year-old is left-handed, just like his father. He looks so much like him. It's like his father come back from the dead."

I myself knew the father only slightly, he died suddenly of a heart attack, when this son was a year old. Now the kid is just out of the air force and has come back to see his grandmother, who he has not seen since he was a baby. The mother for some reason has withheld all information about the father.

"So," the chief says, "I got out the father's personnel file. All the pictures we had of him. All the different memos and letters of commendation. I told him the good and the bad about his father."

I'm lying here wondering what the bad was, and why it was necessary to tell.

On his way out the chief bends over me, and says, "Hurry back, everybody misses your cheerful face and sardonic comments."

I guess it is a good exercise for me to have visitors. But I don't want to. I am in such burning discomfort all the time that I just lie around. For a solid week all I do is watch TV. It's tolerable at night, but in the long draggy hours of the morning and afternoon there is nothing you want to see. The soap operas rot your brain. When I was young, we didn't have television, we didn't get a TV set until 1957, the last family in the neighborhood. So I was quite a reader as a boy. I read all the Bomba the Jungle Boy books and Clair Bee's whole Chip Hilton series.

I tell Sydney she's a brainy professor and knows what I'd like, so give me something to read. She says a big strong fellow like me should go for Ernest Hemingway. That appeals. I've heard a lot about Hemingway. So she has me read two things, a short story called "The

Short Happy Life of Francis Macomber" and a novel, *A Farewell to Arms*. I go nuts over both of them. I wonder why I gave up my youthful habit of reading. I especially enjoy the part in the short story where he actually goes into the mind of the lion. And in the novel I whip along like a bandit when they are rowing across the Swiss lake. I forget my butt and become totally involved in the action. I see why the name of Hemingway is so honored.

But Sydney sits down on the bed beside me and says, "Don't you think Hemingway's women characters are too simple? The castrating bitch in the short story, the devoted doll in the novel."

I say I wouldn't know, not being acquainted with his other writings. But as to the first type, there really are women like that running around in the world. I've known a couple. I say, "And look at Dick slaving away on that *Othello* paper for English. Iago ain't a slur on Italians. Stories got to have their villains, right?"

We kind of bat the ball back and forth. She says, "Catherine is every man's fantasy of the yielding female. Totally absorbed in her man's life. She never gives a thought to her own."

I think about that. I say, "I'd like a little time just to enjoy what I read. Why pick it apart?"

She says, "You're a typical freshman. They think analysis is the enemy of beauty."

I say, "I would never say analysis is the enemy of beauty, dear. I analyze you all the time, and it only makes you more beautiful. So there. And don't call me a freshman. Bad enough I'm wearing a diaper. I don't need to wear a beanie."

She pats my hand.

I say, "Isn't it important that Catherine dies at the
end of the story? Frederick Henry is telling us about the
woman he loved who died. He doesn't want to say anything critical about her or show her in a bad light. As you
always do with a person who has died. You don't dishonor
their memory. You told me Hemingway called this book
his *Romeo and Juliet*. Would Romeo dump on Juliet?"

"No," she says, kind of smiling.

"It's like on a date when you take a girl out you
want to be sort of courtly and soft-spoken and have your
words mean more than they say. And when you're in love
you're blind to all the little faults of a person. What's
wrong with that? Besides, Frederick Henry shows us how
she was all vulnerable and fucked up when he first met
her."

Sydney looks away, and mutters, half to herself,
"Like I was when you met me."

That stops us for a moment, as we remember the
circumstances in which we met. She's never talked about
it. Now she hurries by it, she says, "When they make
love in the hospital, Catherine does all the work. He just
lies there."

I blurt out, "His kneecap's blown away!" Then we
both get embarrassed. Given my predicament, we haven't
fooled around since the operation.

But just talking with her like this is a real thrill for
me. Reading a good book and trading ideas about it. This
is what I missed out on by not going to college. This is
what I want for Dick. It is stimulating, ta-da. Makes you
less at the mercy of all the bullshit of life. And it's not
just superficial chitchat when we do it.

So that picks up my spirits. What gets me on my

feet, however, and back into the world again, is something that hardly brightens my outlook. I get a phone call from the chief. I was afraid of this, I could kind of see it coming. Walter Wright, one of our finest officers, commits suicide. Excellent man. The type of guy who had to have everything in its own little spot. He'd go over all his paper work until it was perfect. Nothing could be messy or out of place. He'd always return a patrol car absolutely clean inside and out. His uniforms spotless, the creases in his pants just right, an ex-military person. When his wife took their daughter and disappeared, he couldn't handle the mess of it, the stress and strain, and he went off the deep end.

Over the phone the chief says, "When I went into the house, it was just like when Walter was alive. Uniforms neatly hung in the closet, shirts stacked on the dresser, all his IDs and personal items and his collar brass laid out perfect. He used one bullet, through the heart. The other five were lined up evenly."

So I pull myself together, go down to the mortuary and stand honor guard. White gloves. The flag on the casket, the top half open, Walter lying there in uniform. You don't smile or cry or look at the floor, just stare straight ahead, no emotion in your face. It's difficult when people try to talk to you. At the funeral service we stand at ease in front of the casket and stare straight ahead again right over the tops of heads, the place is packed. At the end, grandparents and friends and children and cousins and nieces pass by. It is awfully somber. All the pallbearers are officers, and we put me in the middle of the strong side, I'm not yet up for heavy lifting. We carry the casket out to the hearse, and then at the cemetery we carry it from the hearse to the grave. They play taps, the final salute. I hate it when they give the flag to the widow. She was the reason he shot himself.

Sydney's dinner party idea starts out as part of her Triphammer Reclamation and Rehabilitation Project. And, also, she thinks it'll be a good test of our ability as a twosome to dive into the social swim. For some time, even before my operation, she's been complaining that we are too housebound, not meeting each other's friends. I don't have the heart to tell her how short my list is.

We decide to start small, just one other couple. She picks out her half of the deal, a woman she's just met, Julie Katzen. Julie's a lecturer in the psychology department. Syd says Julie is a lonely soul and could use a dinner out.

For my side I can't come up with anyone right away. I don't want to invite the chief. Judy Cook would throw the table off balance in more ways than one. I think a lot about it, and there's no one I really want to invite. I see how alone I am in this world. Finally I decide I want someone more Syd's age than mine, so that it won't be like two different generations staring at each other in a Mexican standoff. I settle on Ted Vandermark, our youngest officer. A couple of years ago his wife had a baby, and every time the baby did something new, we all got to hear a drawn-out story about it in the locker room. Like none of the rest of us had ever had children. Now his wife has left him, taking the baby, and Ted has been moping around the station like Walter Wright, nervous and twitchy, hitting the hootch at night and reporting for duty all hung over. He's tickled to death when I invite him. Big kid, a weight lifter, carrot top. So I think both Syd and I have used a social occasion to reach out to people in trouble. That thought pleases me, as we plan for it. I ask Dick to join us, but he decides to sidestep the social whirl. He'll spend the evening with a bunch of kids at Becky's house; they are planning an all-nighter, a sensitivity session. I caution him about getting too sensitive. He says in this supercool saxophone-player black voice, "What it *is*, man. And shit."

All day Saturday Syd and I prepare. She goes ape in my little kitchen, uses every pot and pan I have. I go to the A & P and get steaks, steaks being simple. I get the butcher to butterfly me some excellent tenderloin. Sydney wants to start with steamed clams, so I pick up two dozen of those at the fish store. She herself has bought a ton of fresh beans, and multicolored pasta, and now she's making two different salads, and this mashed carrot dish that she says is excellent but which seems to me entirely too much effort, and chocolate cake. She's making mistake number one. Way too elaborate. I say, "You got to walk before you can run." She says, "You don't have a spice in the house."

She's surrounded herself with cookbooks, and says she wishes she were in a real kitchen, her own. We should be doing this at the Carriage House. I am reduced to Head Dishwasher and Errand Boy, running out for things she forgot. At six, I set the table. I hardly mention my butt, which is fiercely hurting. But she has forgotten all about me, she's into endive.

Julie Katzen is the first to show up, and at first she strikes me as a kind of cartoon of Sydney. Tall and dark, wearing this baggy man's suit she must've gotten at a thrift shop, and high heels. I guess I look at her funny because right away she's crestfallen. She stares down at her suit and says, "Oh." I pretend not to have looked at her whatever way I did. Sydney has dressed calmly, for her, in a simple black sleeveless dress. Now Julie Katzen looks at her as if to say, You don't dress like that at school—is that who you are at home with your cop? Or maybe I am just paranoid. I'm already sweating up my own clothes. I ask Julie to help me select the dinner music. We go into the living room, and she looks through my record collection. She says, "Mozart from *Time-Life*?" Shit, I love those records. Now I feel like a tasteless numbskull. I leave her sitting on the floor and go back into the kitchen where I see Syd's pissed that Julie has brought us a little bottle of Remy Martin cognac. She puts the Remy under the sink with the Joy.

A half hour later, after I've begun to wonder where the hell he is, Ted shows up. He looks about twelve years old in a forest green sport coat that doesn't exactly match his Jamesway golf green slacks. He has clearly fortified himself before coming, and he's carrying a big bottle of Gallo Hearty Burgundy, which he sets down on the dining room table. He says, "A little Dago red to liven up the proceedings."

I wonder if this bottle is destined for Detergent Land too, and before Syd can store it, I grab glasses and pour.

She glances at me, and I whisper to her, "It's rude not to drink the wine your guests brought, isn't it?"

She says, "No, and you're out of salt."

When we finally get ourselves seated at the dinner table and start eating, I catch telltale signs that all has not gone well in the kitchen. The green beans are more like a garnish than a dish. She burned them up. Each of us gets three singed beans. The French bread I bought does not make an appearance, either. I guess it was part of the general conflagration. My kitchen smells like a German city in 1944 after an Allied bomber run. Finally, when smoke begins to waft out into the dining room, I go in there and find an empty pan's bottom coalescing into the burner. I grab the pan and throw it out into the garage. I bring up a little fan from the basement. I try to be unobtrusive.

Julie has to have her steak well done, so I put it back in and ruin it. Syd, Julie, and I take turns trying to make conversation. We fail. Then Ted takes a shot at it. He says that Harry Kramnick has died. Harry was ninety, and everybody in the neighborhood loved him. With this philosophical look on his face, Ted says, "Jewish. But a hell of a nice old guy."

Everything stops. Dead silence.

I immediately look to my left at Sydney, and a dark cloud has passed over her face. I look across the table, over the candles, and Julie can't believe her ears. She stares at her plate. I pour more wine. The candles themselves won't cooperate, the fan stirs up the air so that the red wax blows down in puddles on the white cloth.

We just eat. Carve and chew. No lively talk. Just the low clatter of knives and forks on dishes. I look to my

right, at Ted, and across the table at Julie—they're me
and Syd. A woman professor and a man cop. Not possible.
Won't compute. The carrot dish is actually very good. I
compliment Syd on her cooking. She looks at me as
though I'm being sarcastic.

Over salad Syd tells Julie how touched she is by
Dickie. He's so eager and sweet, so mystified by the big
world, so unprepared for it. Julie nods, "Freud says that
the education we give our children to face the world is
like giving a map of the Swiss lakes to a polar expedi-
tion."

Out of nowhere—we'd almost forgotten about him—
Ted says, "Fuckin' A."

Oh well, with our fresh-ground coffee and chocolate
cake, we just sit and endure the time we must spend here
on earth. Finally I clap Ted on the back, and he and I go
into the living room. We sit down heavily, him in my
black Barcalounger and me on the couch. I think that if
only Syd and I could be better together, and gather our
wits about us, maybe Julie Katzen and Ted Vandermark
could exchange the sorrow of what has been hurting
them. They could have an okay evening and maybe even
learn something. But it's all scorched earth now. The two
women join us—that is, they come into the room and sit
down at the other end. With my eyes I keep signaling to
Syd for help, but she doesn't get my message. She pulls
my little oak rocking chair over beside Julie, and they
blab away about college shit. Ted gets fainter and fainter.
I think we may lose him. The horrible evening drags on
like an old dog with the mange. I go into the kitchen,
reach down under the sink, and get the cognac. I pour a
lot of it into two big brandy snifters and bring them in.

Ted laps it up. He babbles on to me in this low pathetic voice about how his wife has torn his heart out. Women are no damned good. At one point he breaks out of his sob story and laughs. He says last week on duty he answered a call to this domestic. "The man was drunk as a goose," he says. He drains his brandy snifter and just sits there.

"Yes?" I say. "And?"

He looks at me. "Oh," he says. "This guy was going to leave his wife—and take the TV with him. Was trying to cut the cable with a nutcracker. A fuckin' nutcracker." Ted laughs again. And then he stops. Suddenly he stands up. His face as green as his clothes. He looks around wildly. Starts to walk. Stops. Says, "I think I need to lie down."

I think he does too. I help him down the hall into the guest room. He falls onto the bed. I take off his shoes. He's out like a light. I sit beside him on the edge of the bed. He's through.

I come back to the living room, where Syd is looking at me like it's all my fault. Syd and Julie go outside on the porch. I'm wondering if the Duke and Duchess of Windsor ever had evenings like this. I go out and sit on the porch with them, and we smoke cigarettes. Julie and Syd are talking about Freud's theory of penis envy. I must make some kind of a "Humph!" sound because Julie turns to me and smiles this faint little smile. "Yezz?" she says.

I say I don't really know a thing about it. But why couldn't this theory of penis envy mean that little boys had all the advantages and little girls couldn't see why? Little girls in the tub with their brothers could find no differences except one. She doesn't actually envy the penis, little bit of tissue. But it's the only difference she can see. What's wrong with Freud's idea?

Julie Katzen looks at me in my porch light. She says, "How much time do I have?"

"Oh, forget it," I say. I feel bad about poor Ted.

Julie has been staring at me, however, and now she says, "You're not as dumb as you look."

I say, "I try not to be."

The whole evening is such a spectacular failure that I'm kind of enjoying it now. Like this movie Syd and I watched on the VCR, *The Treasure of the Sierra Madre*. At the end, when you have lost everything, you might as well laugh. Nothing much else you can do. I kind of like Julie Katzen. She's very fragile, easily hurt. I'm sorry we haven't provided a good evening for her. She looks pale.

I go back inside. Eventually I hear Julie drive away.

Sydney and I are not able to recover. She says I have been a bad host. Drinking. We sit in the living room. Syd's got a big glass of ice water, and I am finishing Julie's cognac. I know that every dish in the house is waiting for me in the sink and all over the drainboards.

I say, "Honey, why am *I* the bad host? You ignored Ted—completely ignored him."

She looks at me hot.

I say, "He was *your* guest too. At least I tried with Julie. But you slammed the door in Ted's face."

"After all the crap he said? What am I —?"

"He's just going through a bad time."

"He is, indeed."

"Well," I say, "I hope you don't treat your students this way. Some of them must say pretty ignorant things.

No reason to cast them out. You got to reach out to them. Don't just blame people for their personal problems."

Oh boy, she does not appreciate my high-handed wisdom at all. She says, "Shut up. You're drunk."

I say, "No, I'm not."

Syd says, "You knew Ted was loaded when he got here. And you just poured more liquor down him. You're not his friend."

She has tried to do a good thing. Work all day over a hot stove, then have the whole evening flop, and now me giving her a hard time.

We sit here, like fighters in their corners. Finally I go squat down at my record player and put on *Time-Life* Mozart. I think it is very pretty. I return to my chair, sit back, and watch the cognac roll and glide in the snifter in my palm. I love the all-over warm feeling this stuff gives me. I say, "Jesus, Syd, let's not fight."

She looks away.

I say, "I'm sorry about Ted. But he didn't mean anything. His wife left him and took his kid. The guy doesn't know what hit him."

"Well," she says. "I know what's hitting me. You."

"C'mon. Don't."

"Fuck you."

I look at her, her brown eyes flushed with tears.

I have many things on my mind. And do not say them.

She gets up and walks over to me. She stands here in her basic black dress, towering over me, her hair kind of wild. Slowly she pours her glass of ice water all over my lap. Then she goes back to the oak rocker, grabs her purse, and walks out into the night. I listen to her out there in the driveway in her Honda. She finally gets the poor thing started, and she goes chugging away.

I sit here all soggy. Actually, I'm soaked through. I finish the cognac. Then I get up and take off my pants and go bare-legged into the disaster area of the kitchen. I do dishes and pots and pans and bowls. I whistle a happy tune. The phone rings. My heart skips a beat, and I toddle down to the phone on the wall, pick up the receiver, and say, "Hi, beautiful, come on back."

There's a pause and then Julie Katzen says, "Gee, I'd love to."

That startles me. Is she kidding or what? I say, "Oh, hello."

We chat a little. She's sorry Syd's gone. She says she feels bad she was such a drag and spoiled the party. I say no, of course not, we'll try again soon. I say, "Why don't you give Syd a call? She'd probably like to talk."

Julie says, "Yup."

I dry some dishes. I imagine Sydney lying awake in that bed of hers in the Carriage House. Real upset. I'd love to sneak in and surprise her, all quiet, it's over, here I am. Take her in my arms.

Around six, in my own bed, I look up and Ted is shaking me by the shoulder. We have coffee at the dining room table. He's badly hung over. I try to see the good in him. He says his wife has left him now, but she gave him the greatest gift a woman can ever give a man, her virginity. As he stammers on, I begin to see that he doesn't really care about his actual loss. Certainly not his kid. This is all just an insult to his masculinity. I think he's not too smart. I think he should straighten up and not be a fool. I blow on my coffee, and I think of a word Syd has taught me to ponder—"inane." Ted Vandermark, in the cold light of dawn, seems to me pretty inane.

When Dick was born, I was twenty-eight and Sheila was twenty-four. I had it fixed in my mind firmly that I wanted a family and all the things that go with it. I thought Sheila and I were in agreement on that. We were poor as two church mice. I was a patrolman, ninety-six bucks a week. The only previous full-time job I had had was in a dental lab making false teeth. When I became a police officer, I worked from midnight to eight. Never took money out of my checks for myself. I gave it all to Sheila. Never had money in my pocket. Walking the beat, I couldn't even stop in somewhere for a cup of coffee or a sandwich. I used to drop into the diner at two or three o'clock when they'd throw away the food that was left on the steamtable, and Nick'd give me something. Sheila never cooked for me at all; she was too busy doing other things. After working all night, I'd come home starving and find no breakfast. So I'd go out and work somewhere. A policeman by night and a jack-of-all-trades by day. I painted houses, went back to my old gas station, cleaned up restaurants and bars—anything anybody wanted done, I would do it. Averaged about four hours sleep a day. But we were making it, we had our own little piece of land, and we put a trailer on it, hoping that someday it would be a house. Sheila decided she wanted to go to work, so she took a job as a secretary over at the new junior college. It was a two-year institution then, before it became a regular branch of the state system. She didn't make great money, but she banked it all, and she paid the bills out of my paycheck.

She was not too happy to have a policeman for a husband. Not too happy about anything I did. Married life was not what she had been led to expect. After the courting period she never seemed to enjoy our sex life very much. Always blamed it on me. Said I couldn't make her happy in bed. Gradually I got browbeaten to the point where all my self-confidence went down the tubes. When you are never sure of yourself, you become overly careful of everything you say and do, trying to make things better. Which only makes them worse.

Her mother and grandmother were very strict Baptists. Or so they purported to be. Sheila herself seemed to have an on-again, off-again thing with the church. On weekends while I'd work somewhere, she'd ask for the car and she and Dickie would go to her grandmother's. I thought it was probably a good idea for her to spend time with the family. Her dad had died when she was only four years old. He died right in front of her eyes, in the kitchen. He was fixing his little girl lunch and dropped dead. Sheila was alone with his body until her mother came home from work at six. How the hours must have dragged by. I guess she kept trying to wake him up; a four-year-old has no concept of death. It probably affected her very seriously and remained tucked there in her unconscious mind.

We had been married for seven years when all of a sudden these little things started to come up. Stories did not check out. Unexplained absences. On weekends when I call the grandmother, she says she doesn't know where Sheila is. And she's out sick at her secretarial job, though I had noticed no sickness at home. There is all this time unaccounted for. So one night I finally faced her with it. I was standing there in the trailer, and I said, "I demand an explanation." Probably the first time in her life Sheila was speechless. She had this very strange half-fearful, half-angry look on her face. Pouty. After a bit she admitted she had been seeing her girlfriend's husband.

I went into a rage. I said, "You can go fuck yourself!" I went out, got into the car, and drove away. Went down to a bar and got wadded. I must have had eight or nine drinks in two hours' time. Didn't make me feel any better. I tried to figure out why my whole world was coming unraveled when I had thought it was all a neat little package. Went home to the trailer and couldn't even go into bed. I slept on the couch. Where I began to sleep permanently. From then on, all we had were a lot of arguments. Every night I'd go out and get drunk. I had worked my ass off, and now I could see everything all just like a vapor going away from me. I could not handle it. Come home snockered every night. I was not exactly polite or even pleasant. I wasn't sure whether she was still seeing this guy. She said she wasn't. But I kind of lost track and quit all my extra jobs. I didn't care whether there was any money in the checkbook or not.

One night, very late, she came into the trailer where I was sitting in my shorts drinking beer. She said, "I'm going to move to Buffalo."

I said, "You what?"

"I'm getting my own apartment," she said. "And I'm taking Dickie with me."

I had never even thought about losing Dickie.

"I've found a place," she said. "Uncle Buck is going to help me move. What of our stuff do you want?"

I said, "I don't care what you take." I thought about it a little, and then I said, "I want the new TV." I don't know why. You can't sleep on a TV. Can't even sit on it.

I wasn't sure when the day was coming. I kept on drinking. I used to carry cases of beer in the trunk of my car, and if anybody said party, I'd flip the trunk open and we'd party right there. But one day I came home and the trailer was empty except for that TV. And it sank in that I was absolutely alone.

I didn't care about losing her, but I really missed Dickie. I was a lost soul. Really got into the booze. For about a year. One weekend per month I'd drive to Buffalo and bring Dickie home. It was a disaster, I couldn't hardly sober up enough to enjoy him. I'd let him go out and play with his old friends; they had a toboggan. I'd watch them play out there in zero weather and I'd drink inside. I didn't have anything good to do with him, his whole little life was in Buffalo now. He wasn't too excited to be with me. In the car he'd just sleep in the backseat.

Eventually I found out that she had squirreled away about seven thousand dollars in bank accounts. Didn't take her long, though, to wipe that out. I guess I figured I'd let her try life on her own, give her a little leeway, and she'd see the errors of her ways. Then we could get back together. If she had asked, I would have taken her back, with the aim of straightening our lives out. Which shows just how dumb I was. Unwilling to face reality.

In the meantime I was out drinking every night. One night in a bar I met a girl and went home with her. Ruthie. Real pretty little redhead, soft and gentle, didn't have a mean bone in her body. One thing led to another, and all of a sudden like a thunderclap, I found out that Sheila's and my sexual problem didn't have to do with me. Being with Ruthie, I finally could see that it was Sheila who had the hangups. And given the number of boyfriends she was going through, I guess she never did work it out. With Ruthie I regained my confidence, and my drinking eased up.

Then one day a deputy calls me. I think he just wants me to come in and have coffee. I go meet him, and lo and behold, the son of a bitch serves me with a summons. Family court. Appear on such and such a date at such and such a time. To establish a separation agreement and child-support payments. Made me furious. Sheila could have simply told me. I had been paying support voluntarily. But the judge took 25 percent of my salary plus I had to pay all the medical and dental bills. Every time on the job when I'd get a raise, I'd get a petition from Buffalo to up the payments. For a while there I was permanently broke. Finally Sheila charged *me* with adultery. I fought the piss out of that one. I cross-filed for mental cruelty. Things dragged out. I found it awfully strained with Dickie. I think his mother filled him up with stories against me. It hurt me to see the look in his eyes, like he was checking me out against the version of me that his mother had given him. I have little doubt that she told him I was a worthless drinker. And I wasn't giving him much to contradict her. When I'd get loaded, his gray eyes seemed to say, Yep, Mom told me about this.

But her life was no bowl of cherries. One night when I drove up there to Buffalo and returned Dickie to her, she kept me a while and made up this cock-and-bull story. During the course of the discussion she said, "Trip, maybe we could get back together again and try to make a go of it."

But I sensed she had been rejected by a lover, or somebody she'd been going with had decided he wanted something different. It was pretty obvious to me that she was just between boyfriends. Or she had been through something very trying. She was very flirtatious with me. Put on soft music. Lights down low. She tried to get me into bed. But I did not want to get entangled in the same old goddamn mess. I went home to Ruthie. That relationship did me a world of good. I was enjoying things I never enjoyed before. Ruthie and I had a good sex life, got along well together, and if I'd come home late, she'd actually fix me something good to eat.

I hated Christmas. Homes all lighted up, everybody happy, or so they appeared. The worst Christmas was when Dick was about six. I always used to take him a whole bunch of gifts to try to make up for not having him. So this Christmas I drove up to Buffalo, my car full of presents, and I took an armload up to her apartment door. After I knocked, she answered in a bathrobe. Kind of sheepish and confused. I said, "Are you going to let me in, or are you going to let me freeze to death here with my arms full of presents?" She lets me in. As I walk over toward the tree, I see this guy sleeping on the couch. I stop. I stand there staring at him. It is the first time I have actually seen another man in her home. But as usual, I felt it was my fault, I felt I was the intruder.

I put the presents down. Dick was asleep in his bedroom. I went back out for another load. When I come back in, this idiot on the couch wakes up. And he's plastered. I tried to slough it off. I really didn't want Dickie to wake up. I tried to be careful of my responses. I explained I was just dropping off presents. But this guy is going fuck this and fuck that, getting loud. I was ready to tap the dude aside his head. So finally he comes over and shoves me and tells me to get out. That is the last straw. I grab him by the seat of the pants and the scruff of the neck. I throw him right out the screen door. He bounces off the first step, and they had a landing down there and a second set of steps. I think I broke his arm; there was a big lump sticking out above his elbow. I'm not sure he knew it was broken, but he knew it hurt. He started to come back up the icy steps, and I went down and stood there and told him that if he knew what was good for him, he'd keep right on trucking. I was livid. He went out and got in his car and drove away.

Sheila was just sitting there in a rocking chair with this dumb look on her face. I left all the rest of the presents under the tree and got out of there. Dickie didn't wake up. And the boyfriend never did sue me or try to collect any money off me. But that was the night I knew we'd never have a chance again.

We went ahead with the divorce. It was easy; we just got the lawyers to draw up the papers and the judge did it on his noon hour. My attorney was there with me, her attorney didn't show up, Sheila didn't show up. So it was uncontested. I got on the stand and testified. The judge asked me if the marriage could ever be repaired or was the damage too severe. I said the damage was too severe. He slammed his little gavel, said, "Divorce granted," and I went on my way. Fifteen minutes.

So my family was ruined. I'd never get a chance to participate in Dickie's growing up, never get the opportunity to mold his future, never get to be a part of his little victories and defeats. I tried once to get custody, but it never even came to court. It got squashed in preliminaries. I thought I could have him a year, she could have him a year, but she wouldn't hear of that. It never got off the ground. She had brainwashed me over the years, and I had persuaded myself it was all my fault. Mom was very observant of that. She never liked Sheila. Tolerated her, tried to be friendly to her, but never felt comfortable with her because of the way she treated me. Mom said I moped around like a whipped puppy. My head down. Never had confidence in myself, always seemed to be unhappy about something.

So I limped along by myself, seeing Dick when I could. Then things in Buffalo started to deteriorate. Sheila looked terrible, lost a lot of weight—and began calling me in the middle of the night. I could tell she was not exactly in her right mind. I blamed it on the pills her new doctor was giving her. Goofy pills, they turned her into a motor mouth. Even the guy she finally settled on called me a few times to ask me if she was this way when we were married. He was pretty much a sad sack himself and not too bright. I do not think at that time I really understood amphetamines, but her therapist was giving her all these "uppers" to counteract her terrible depressions and fearfulness. I was so angry I just kept telling myself it was her turn to suffer. I was kind of glad to see her in pain, after all the pain she had put me through.

And then one January day the call came. Her boyfriend said he had come home for lunch to find the apartment filled with the smell of carbon monoxide. Of course carbon monoxide is odorless, but he didn't know that. They lived over the garage. The boyfriend said he found her body on the first floor landing. He opened all the windows that he could open and called the police, and she was not responsive to CPR. He had no idea she'd do what she did, even after some strange episodes that maybe were other attempts. She had this cherry pink flush on her skin, he said, and drool from her lips. She had started the car, like she was going shopping, but she didn't take her purse, her purse was back in their bedroom. We never did figure out why she was on the landing. Maybe she realized that she had started the car and was going back down to turn it off. Was she going to or from the car? Maybe she felt herself being overcome and was trying to escape. I dropped everything and drove up there. Dickie was at school, and we arranged to have a friend pick him up and keep him overnight.

They ruled it a suicide. I think a key was some letters they found which indicated she was leaning that way. She had mentioned the possibility to her psychologist. In his report he said she was suffering from this thing called agoraphobia. A morbid dread of being in the midst of open space. Maybe it caught up with her after she started the car, and she couldn't go out into the world.

I went over to the friend's house, got Dickie, and brought him home. He was just shy of his eighth birthday. I did not want him ever to go back there, where sooner or later he'd hear that his mother killed herself. I broke all the connections. Her boyfriend didn't seem to mind. Dickie only went back to Buffalo once, for the funeral, where I stuck to him like glue. The story I concocted and told him was that a little place in her brain went bad, and she died instantly. It was a terrible ordeal he went through when I told him, and I'm not sure I did it right. At the funeral I made sure the casket was closed. I didn't want him to remember her that way. Especially if they couldn't fix the cherry pink color. I figured he'd have enough nightmares.

It took him a long time to work out his grief. I spent long hours and days and weeks trying to help him with it. For a while he was just obsessed with this one aspect; he'd bang his fist on his little leg and say, very determined, "I wish I could remember the last thing I said to her." It was like he couldn't let go. Like it was a way to keep her alive and not really bury her. Or maybe it was like he thought it was his fault, that if he had said something else she might still be alive. I don't know. I'd think he was through with that line of thought, and then it would come back again, always with that little bang of his fist on his leg. I wonder if he suspected. I stuck to my story that it was a little blood vessel in the brain.

I didn't want my son to grow up in a trailer. So I sold it, got a loan, mortgaged myself way in over my head, and got this house. Dickie and I began our life together.

I see Sheila very differently now. Not like I saw her during all the agony of the divorce. I was too angry to pick up on what was really happening. I think a lifelong thing was breaking through, all the underlying fear coming to the fore. Everything caved in on her. I say that that is what happened to me, but it was much more true for her. Obviously. Things look so different to me now. Like when I threw her drunk boyfriend down the stairs that Christmas. I say she sat in the rocking chair with a stupid look on her face. It wasn't just stupid. It was mental illness. I see that face in my dreams. And what about "agoraphobia"? Why did Sheila have a fear of open spaces? Maybe she had a fear of closed spaces. I keep coming back to her father dying in the kitchen and her being alone with the body all those long hours. I thought she didn't cook for me because of laziness and indifference. But maybe kitchens were totally off limits emotionally. She spent as little time as possible in the kitchen; she'd always tear through there, even when unloading groceries. Maybe a kitchen brought back her father. In spite of the fact that she always bad-mouthed my job, I wonder if she didn't marry me because I was a policeman. A figure of authority, supposed to provide security. I say I was the injured party, I was the lost soul. But it was Sheila who had been injured, long before she met me. She was the lost soul. Sometimes I get kind of callous, and I say anybody who'd marry me would have to have mental problems. But my heart is no longer hard toward her. In all her frantic running around, she was not really a thrill-seeker. She was probably trying to find safety and comfort. Who knows? Whenever I speak about her to Dick, I try to be gentle and kind. Not as an act. In my dreams about her she is in such a state, frightened, confused. She is both sitting down and in motion.

I wonder if there is any way that I could have been smarter, when I was so young and relatively unconscious.

Could I have seen through her behavior to her real difficulties? No other man seems to have done so. Sheila was
probably beyond help. But then I think of how little help
I was to Patsy Pullman when Kitty was in such dire
straits. I bungled the friendship with Judy Cook. My
failures with women have made me distrustful and wary.
I don't seem to have problems with men. We just get
things done and go about our business. Men are pretty
simple. With women it is always complicated. I wonder,
though, if it isn't them so much as it's me. Some basic
support I fail to provide.

   With Sydney now I am waiting for the other shoe to
fall. I better beat the alcohol; it means so much to her. I
think I can do it. Alcohol was involved in all the failures.
Though more as a result than as a cause. Or maybe I'm
fooling myself about that. Won't know until I try. I do
know that I would give just about anything to have been
able to see Sheila back then the way I see her now. Maybe
our divorce was unavoidable, but it didn't need to be so
nasty. I am sure she had plenty of regret and sorrow. I
had no monopoly on those emotions. Maybe I could have
comforted her. Although I think Sheila was pretty much
unconsolable. I hate to realize the truth, which is that
we put each other through living hell. And put Dickie
through his little version of it. At the funeral he was
completely bewildered. I think right there his eyes got
permanently a shade darker.

I am frantic for signals of progress, like the buds I see on the trees outside my window. They say winter is over and spring is on its way. The chief gives me hope. Sydney ushers the chief out the door, and when she comes back, she tells me he said that what worried him about me on his first visit was that I had the voice of an old man. Now I sound more like myself.

So how your voice sounds is on my mind when Sydney drags me to a cultural affair. The Lit Club at the college has raised money to bring this famous poet, Allen Ginsberg, to come recite. Well, I guess I can go to poetry readings. I am acquiring the earmarks of an educated man. I loved the look on the chief's face when he was telling me about this movie he saw, a dumb comedy, and I said, "I don't waste my time on fluff. Lately I am getting into Italian neorealism." The chief just stared. But it's true. Sydney's been bringing home from the film library all these great old Italian movies like *La Strada* and *Shoeshine* and *The Bicycle Thief*, and we put them on the VCR every night. I'm beginning to get the hang of them. So I guess I am now ready to branch out into hippie poetry. I've heard a little about this Ginsberg. Syd shows me a couple of his books. She shows them to Dick, too, and he tags along with us.

Dick has been playing this little game with Sydney, pretending he can't memorize this teeny-tiny poem she likes, "The Red Wheelbarrow." It ends with "the white chickens." Dick gets all the way through it, and then says, "the white pigeons."

Sydney says, "Chickens, Dick, chickens."

He says, "Who cares? Birds." But he winks at me, he's teasing her. I have noticed for some time now how well they are getting along. They're thick as thieves.

She gives us this little preview of Mr. Ginsberg, a rant and ravy book called *Howl* and a long poem called "Kaddish," about his poor insane mother. It touches me. It reminds me of my mom, even though this is a pretty far cry from the poetry we read back in high school in the fifties. You can't buy a rhyme. And it hardly lifts the soul to the contemplation of higher things. When we go over to the big fellowship room in the student union, the place is packed. Ginsberg has a beard, of course, but he is wearing a sport coat and a striped tie. I guess I had expected him to be in some sort of lavish robes like a guru. College kids are sitting in all the aisles on the floor and up on the stage at his feet, pretty excited just to be in his presence. He carries on for about an hour, reading some poems about hanging out in a supermarket in California and finding a flower in a junkyard. All the while I am checking out Dick in his granny glasses, all intent and caught up in it. Why does this boy not want to go to college?

Ginsberg reads this long homosexual poem about anal sex with a seventeen-year-old boy. We hear a bit more than we bargained for about the thrill of a sphincter loosening. My own poor asshole can hardly bear it. And

the college kids get very, very quiet; they are hushed.
Here they came to hear about the radical peace move-
ment, and now they are getting this leisurely sojourn into
Downtown Sodomy. I sneak a glance or two at Dick,
wondering what he is making of it. When Ginsberg
finishes, the whole room breathes a collective sigh of
relief. He probably won't get an invitation to perform in
the White House. But I actually kind of enjoy it. Sydney
has opened me up to things that in my normal former
mind I would've just dismissed without a second
thought. I would've kissed off this faggot nonsense with
a rather huffy tsk-tsk. But right in the middle of it I
realize I am having a good time. It's interesting. Allen
goes to town with this funny little red accordion-type
thing he plays. He sings for about ten minutes and gets
all the rest of us to sing with him, just one line over and
over and over, "And all the hills ech-o-ing." The whole
room chanting it until you're slightly hypnotized. I think
Dick is surprised to sit here next to his father the cop,
and hear my voice—not an old man's voice, my real
voice—singing along with all the others. I'm pretty surprised myself. I'm going Oh Lord in my brain, my fingers
intertwined with Sydney's. I can't wait to tell the chief.

Ginsberg finishes up with this little P.S. to *Kaddish*,
about how he stumbles upon his insane mother in the
afterlife in a big brass bed in a brick alley. They sit and
talk, mother and son. I make a mental note to tell Mom
about it next time I go out to the cemetery for one of our
little chats.

After the applause all the kids go swarm around
Allen. Sydney runs into one of her students, Mr. Eilenberger, who is high as a kite, and he's clutching some

yellow lined paper, which is a letter from Allen. Mr. Eilenberger wrote to him asking for advice about life and poetry and received back this long letter about Breath.

On the way back to the car Dick's hopping around on the mushy, thawing ground, he's full of the spirit of the evening. He asks us, "Was the sixties really like that?"

I say to him, "You're asking the wrong people—I was too old for the sixties, and Sydney was too young."

Dick says he thinks that anal sex poem was "really brave"—he says it twice—"really brave."

We spin home pretty happy in 1 GROUCH. We sit for a full hour at the dining room table and talk the evening over. Dick recites "The Red Wheelbarrow" perfect, he says "chickens." Allen mentioned it. I look at a page of *Kaddish* again. Sydney has this small placid grin on her kisser. We drink little cups of herbal tea in candlelight. I am astonished at how happy I am, just sitting here with the two people I love most in the world. Why did I fight feelings like this for so long? Or is my brain turning to mush? All the hills are ech-o-ing. The mighty beat of the Triphammer is little tippy-taps. I look at Sydney's face in the candlelight. I am overcome by her loveliness to the point where I quietly go in and secretly take the phone off the hook, just like I'd always do during the daytime when we want no interruptions. It's idiotic to do it at midnight. But I'm hearing a different drummer, I'm into areas I hardly know what to do with. When I return to the candlelit table, both Dick and Sydney look startled, like I have intruded on a secret. "What?" I say. They look like I caught them. *"What?"* They just smile. Even just a year ago I would have felt very uneasy and pushed to be let in on it. Now I figure, Let them have their little confidential shit. I'm not the head of the household, I'm just one of three.

Maybe it's the surgery, and all the pain that has followed. Maybe it's not putting in my eight hours every day and seeing what a garbage dump the world really is. I suppose there will be a day of reckoning. I will return to my senses. But for now I will let things ride. I am Ferdinand the Bull, out in the pasture smelling flowers.

Dick yawns and calls it a night. He kisses us both. Sydney and I sit in the candlelight, not saying much. Finally I clear my throat and I say, just like a teenager, "Wow."

Sydney looks at me. She says, "The chief's right. Your voice is back." She says, "Trips, you remember when you said my sexiest part was my eyes?"

I nod.

"Well, your sexiest part is your voice."

"My voice?"

"Yes," she says, "it's so full of sadness and loneliness. It says I'm missing something, but I don't quite know what it is."

"My voice says that?"

She says, "It was the first thing that attracted me to you."

That makes me all self-conscious. I can hardly talk. I want my voice to be that way, whatever way it is, and I'm too aware of it to do it naturally. So we blow out the candle and go in to bed. We gradually get out of our clothes, without talking, and she's standing there in the little half-light of the closet. She turns to me with her nightgown in her hand, and I'm naked, and then we just come together and hold each other for a long time. Just

standing here it is amazing how this deep sexual feeling
like a long-lost best friend comes to life again all through
my body. Her long soft hair and her shoulders and arms.
We stand here ever so long. My dick hasn't been out on
the town for weeks. And now we can hardly bear all the
rush of feeling. We lie down on my bed of pain. And it is
not painful anymore. I gaze into her eyes and see her fear
for me. I see how conscious she is of all I've been through.
She has this look, this desperate desire to please me and
make it easy for me, not the hungry look of striving into
her own desires. For some reason I am big as a house. She
is being gentle with me now like I was gentle with her at
the beginning. It is quite a new experience for me, pretty
new for both of us.

Afterward, she laughs and says it has been so long
since she's heard me moan *that* way, instead of from
pain. Neither one of us gets up to turn off the little light
in the closet, we just drift off into sleep holding each
other, me flat on my back and her on her side with her
face on my throat. I say to my drowsy mind that we can
have this for years to come. Nothing shall stand in the
way.

But just as I'm falling asleep, something does stand in the way. Someone comes to the front door. I hear loud knocking. I wait for whoever it is to go away, but there it goes again. Sydney is a remarkably sound sleeper, and I very carefully get disentangled from her, throw on my robe, and go to the door. It's Wayne Parker. Swell. The chief wants me to come to the office and take some pictures. We've had a shooting. I think, Well, this is Wayne Parker, and he is busting my chops. I start to laugh. I say, "What do you mean, a 'shooting'?" I can't believe he's standing here. He says he is on his way in himself, and they asked him to stop and pick me up since my phone seems to be out of order.

Right. I say I have to shower and shave. Be there in a few minutes. As usual, I am not believing the seriousness of what Wayne Parker says. A shooting.

I go into the bedroom and kiss Sydney without waking her up.

When I get to the office, everybody in the whole department is in. What's going on? The chief tells me to get the camera ready, he wants both color and black and white. We've got a murder on our hands. A guy's shot in the head, and the suspect is loose somewhere out in the community. A teletype is already out. The chief takes

165

me into his office and briefs me. If anybody's got an old man's voice, I think, it's the chief. Because he is an old man. Or beginning to look it, roused out of bed in the middle of the night. What hair he's got left is sticking out in wisps. His color's not good. He looks at me weird, as if I could make this thing not have happened. But it has. A teenager has walked into his parents' bedroom, turned on the light, and shot his father in the head. Then he walked downstairs out of the house, got into their Cadillac, and was gone. The chief says, "We got two officers down at the house now. The mother was lying there asleep, right beside the father. Now she's at a friend's house, getting cleaned up." The chief says, "Jesus, Trip, she had bone chips and blood all over her."

I put on my off-duty weapon and go to the scene. I take pictures of the hallway and the landing. When I go into the bedroom, I am careful not to step on the shell casing—they have it marked, where the gun ejected the shell. It is a big king-size bed, with this huge bloodstain, blood and brain matter up on the headboard. I do a sequence of color pictures. I do the kid's room just in case there's something there that we overlook. I go back to the master bedroom and gather up evidence, the sheet, pillowcases, the bloody nightgown that has been laid out on the soaked mattress. It only takes half an hour. We secure the house. The boy might come back and try for his mother. Apparently he had some long-standing grudge with the father, and recently the father had been making him go to a drug rehab center in Syracuse. He was an LSD freak, had used it for years, and whatever else he got into along the way. He had been there earlier today. His mother says they thought he was making progress, he was responding pretty well to treatment, maybe developing a new attitude about things. But now, out of the blue and without a word, he came into the bedroom and shot the father. He's heavily armed, with at least two handguns and a rifle and plenty of ammunition. I investigate the backyard. The moon is down and it is very dark; every little noise makes the hair on my neck prickle. A patrol car is circling the area constantly, issuing bulletins every ten or fifteen minutes.

The chief posts a guard in the house. Me. I am not aware of having said I am ready to report back for duty. The chief just seems to assume it. So here I am with my off-duty weapon, a .38, and they also leave me a shotgun so as to have a chance against a man with a rifle. With a shotgun you're pretty sure you won't miss. All the outside lights are turned on, all the inside lights turned off. It's kind of beautiful and eerie—outside things have inside shadows. It's very spooky when the wind blows. All the doors are locked, but he has keys to the house, we know that.

It's a big house. Everything tasteful. I think what I usually do in such situations, how years of accumulating wealth and possessions finally is worthless and does not stave off the hand of tragedy. You figure you're all safe and comfy, and in a blinding flash your life is reduced to rubble. I walk through the dark rooms thinking my dark thoughts. Every little noise, every little creak, makes me tense. I am just waiting for something to happen. I enter the sitting room, where the windows face north, and I walk by the first window and look out. No problem. In the second window I see a person with a shotgun, and I swing around to shoot, and it's a mirror, the exact same

size and shape as the first window. A goddamn mirror.
My heart starts to beat again.

After a couple of hours I sit in the family room in a
position where I can watch the front door through an
archway and see him if he comes in and goes upstairs. I
hear this swishing sound. I get up and walk around.
Nothing. I go back and sit on the couch, and there's the
swish again. What the fuck is it? I'm bothered now, the
bastard's in the house. I sit down with my pistol out.
Half an hour, and there's another *swish*. Really gets my
curiosity up. I check all the doors in all the rooms, the
sliding glass door to the deck off the master bedroom.
Locked. I check the attic. And then as I am coming down
the stairs on tippy-toe, I see the biggest cat I've ever seen,
an orange tiger cat, not at all friendly. He darts away and
I hear the *swish* again. I go to where I think the sound
was coming from, out to the service porch. Down in a
little corner there is a sort of cubbyhole with a gizmo
like the iris of a camera. I walk within a foot of it and the
thing opens. I step back and it closes. It's triggered by an
electric eye. It's so the cat can go in and out.

I survive the night. Ted Vandermark relieves me in
the faint light of dawn. He's not too pleased, kind of
grouchy and out of sorts. But he's brought me a Danish
and a big cup of coffee. I'd rather have a drink. I could
really use one. I apologize to Sydney in my mind. Maybe
it's my job that makes me drink. That's a peach, if the
only way I can stop drinking is to quit being a policeman.

When I go back to the station, everybody is still on
duty. The chief orders me to go take pictures of the
autopsy. I have just put in a full shift, and I am in no
mood to go see somebody dissected. But I'm told to do it

and have no choice in the matter. So I reload the camera. Why didn't this happen when I was totally bedridden? The chief gives me that look again, as if I am the only officer who can handle a camera. So I take off up to the morgue. I go down to the big chilly room where it's all set up. There lies the naked father on the table, a tag on his toe. The doc describes the body, white male, age, weight, fully developed. He puts probes in the holes, to show the path of the bullet, one just above the right ear where it went in and the other behind the left ear where it came out. He says that now he will remove the brain.

Carl, the lab assistant, reminds me of the hunchback of Notre Dame. I am unprepared for what they do next, even though I have heard him say that it is a cranial autopsy. With the scalpel he makes an incision above the temple, just like giving a guy a trim, and goes down over the sideburn and back and across, and he stops at the other ear. The skin is all loose, and he peels the scalp over so that all the hair is hanging there in front of the face. Then he takes this little rotary saw and follows the same line, up and over the top of the head, and the skull comes off just like a cap. He removes the brain—he takes the whole brain out and lays it there on the table. Jesus. I take my pictures. The bullet has done relatively little damage to the brain, it is pretty much intact except for the line where the bullet went in and came out. The brain looks pretty together, as far as brains go. Then the doc takes this big knife and starts to slice it just as if he was cutting up a bologna to make a sandwich—quarter-inch-thick slices, each one showing the path and trauma of the bullet as it went through, the destruction of brain material, the bullet expending its energy, smaller damage at the entry and more trauma and destruction at the exit. He saves several slices for the lab.

We go up to the cafeteria for breakfast. The doc offers me a free one on the house, but I refuse his kind offer. Carl, however, piles on scrambled eggs and hash browns and juice and mixed fruit and muffins; it has been a busy morning and he has worked up an appetite.

Back at the station I get a copy of the teletype. We've crammed in there everything we know about this kid, and sent it nationwide. If any lawman should encounter him, he'll have a chance because he'll know what he's dealing with. The boy is armed and extremely dangerous, and probably high on drugs.

Two days go by with no word. Nobody has spotted him. And then we get a teletype from way out in Kansas. Our subject has been involved in a shooting. He's dead. He killed a trooper. There was a big gun battle. They need somebody to identify the boy's body. The chief asks me to go. I say I can't, this one I really can't do. My butt can't take it. The chief is disappointed in me, treats me like a slacker. He says he has always been counting on me to be his right-hand man when situations like this arise. But then he lets slip that the widow's attorney has asked him to go personally. So I wonder why he asked me. Maybe just to put me through the paces and see how I'd do. He's very cranky when I put him on the plane to go identify the body in Topeka.

The next day he calls me and fills me in. He says, "The trooper was a twenty-four-year veteran of the Kansas Highway Patrol. He was on his way in to teach at the academy. Which I gather is the way they spend the last two years of their duty here. The deal is to get the man off the highways and bring him in to help train rookies. He was tooling along the Kansas Turnpike when he saw the boy hitchhiking with a duffel bag. He decided to stop and check him out. He approached the subject and asked for identification. He went back to the patrol car and called in to have a file check run through the computer. He placed the driver's license on the seat and didn't wait for a reply. He walked back to our subject and knelt down to check the duffel bag. That's when the kid shot him through the top of the head."

I don't exactly understand. If both the trooper and the boy were shot dead, how do we know all these details? The chief's voice sounds like it's in the next room, not long distance. I'm waiting for instructions, and I don't know why he is telling me all this. Maybe just to get it off his chest.

"They were just outside the tollbooths. A collector called it in. Other units started to respond. The boy realized what was happening when he heard the sirens. He jumped in the cruiser and took off. The other cruisers went after him; they started coming in from all directions. A chase ensued, involving a helicopter. Finally ended here in downtown Topeka. The boy lost control, broadsided another car, and slid into the apron of a gas station. They had a fifteen-minute shoot-out. When they pulled the boy out of the car, he was still squeezing the gun. Had eleven or twelve holes in him."

Next day the chief brings back a whole bunch of weapons, a small .30-caliber carbine, two handguns, a .32 semiautomatic, which the kid had used to kill both his father and the trooper, and a 9-millimeter Luger. Lots of ammunition. He had no permits, but his father had permits for all of them. I think about how all those weapons were registered to the father.

I think about it staring into my drink. I am very sorry to break my pledge to Sydney, but something in me kind of breaks loose after all the tension. The space seems so vast, from here to Topeka. I get very big oversimplified ideas about America. Try to water them down with alcohol. Which of course makes my ideas seem to me even more profound. I try to make note of what is happening, in hope that maybe this will be the last time. I take some pride in the fact that I don't actually go to a liquor store and buy it. I am just finishing up the rag-tag end of things from the carton at the back of the closet in my den. A parting of the ways, a final good-bye.

I become conscious of a couple of things sitting here staring at the glass. First, the expression "feeling no pain." It is true. I think maybe that is why I have turned to alcohol over the years. Alcohol is when I am alone with my thoughts. It is the only time when I get to all that is behind my daily life. To the assumptions behind everything, to the guiding principles. What you share only with yourself. Stuff that cannot be talked about. It's a way of holding all your feelings together. And pissing them away, of course. It's kind of a oneness with yourself. And other things, too. Like you really want everything in your life to go okay. When you are at a certain point with the booze, it happens. Everything really does seem okay. It's bullshit, and you know that, but you enjoy the feeling. How warm you get. No matter how much you tell yourself it's a coward's way out, your system can really use a pep talk. John Barleycorn doesn't fail you. Not while you're doing it, not while you are actually in there. Only afterward do you realize what a fool you have been.

Except this time it doesn't work because I am so conscious of how disappointed in me Sydney will be. Instead of staggering into bed and falling into blissful sleep, I get angry with myself. Lie here on my back and wish I hadn't done it. Realize I am frightened. Wish I had done what the chief asked me and gone to Topeka. I am not feeling no pain. More the opposite. I finally go under, and wake up all groggy, my head throbbing. I struggle into the bathroom to piss. While I slept, Dick and Syd came home. Now they are both standing there, with very stern looks on their faces. Like a delegation. I crawl beneath the covers, and they let me have it.

Their tone of voice isn't angry. But that makes it even harder on me, like they have gone beyond me and I got to play catch-up. The whole thing makes me uneasy. All I can do is sit here in bed and let it sink in. That I am the problem. That I have been such a disappointment to them that they have had to take steps.

Sydney says, "I've been going to meetings of a group for the family members of alcoholics. Al-Anon. I've been going for weeks. Since before your operation. I don't feel so helpless."

And Dick says he's been going to Ala-Teen. He says, "I just listen to how other kids deal with alcoholic parents."

I'm angry. Two against one. I wish they had told me. Why'd they have to do it behind my back? I'd like the chance to fix it myself. I say so.

Sydney says, "If you could, you already would have.

One of the most destructive myths about compulsive drinkers is that they're not trying hard enough."

I don't know where she got to be such an expert all of a sudden. I say, "I'm not even sure I am an alcoholic. Wait until I slip up again. And then I promise I'll go. But let us see if I have the emotional wherewithal to succeed on my own two feet."

Nothing less than attending AA is good enough for them. I have to take that good-faith first step. And before I know what I am about, I say okay. But I am feeling that something is being taken away from me. Like I am an object to be dealt with.

Dick shakes my hand, to make our promise binding, then goes into his bedroom and turns on his boom box. I sit here pretty defeated. I say to Syd, "I think you have exceeded your authority with regard to Dick. As his father, I should have been consulted. Should have known about this Ala-Teen stuff."

She looks at me sadly. And she tells me a story that really makes me sit up. She says, "He told me about a dream he kept having as a child. It was a nightmare for a long time. A big monster was chasing him, a monsterlike robot, all steel and metal and clanking sounds. But it was furry, too, like a gorilla. It chased him all over and finally got him cornered. Just as it was leaning down to crush him, its headpiece came off and there you were inside, his dad, crying."

I about faint when I hear this dream. My mind flies all over the place, I would give my left testicle for my son never to have had such a dream.

Sydney says, real soft, "You're the first man I've been with who believes in a right way and a wrong way of

living. Not to do something about your drinking is a
wrong way. You can't let it drag on."

I say OK, OK, OK. But I am horrified at my son's
dream. And I can't now make him not have it. I am just
locking the barn door after the horse has been stolen.

I have always pictured Alcoholics Anonymous as
just a bunch of poor lost souls with hangdog faces sitting
around in a church basement telling their troubles to
each other. Lo and behold, that is what it is. In the
basement of the First Presbyterian Church, Tuesday night
at eight-thirty. Sydney's Al-Anon group meets at the
same time in the Fellowship Room.

I recognize a couple of them. I've met them in my
job, pulled them over for DWI, come to their houses
when they went crazy and locked themselves in the
bathroom and wouldn't come out. They don't seem to
recognize me, given the state they were in when we
crossed paths.

The main thing that strikes me about them is their
eyes. They've been through it. Down to the dregs. Eyes
just filled with sadness. But strong eyes. Won't be distracted from their purpose. These eyes have seen it all,
and they don't skitter away, they don't quit on you.

Actually, that is true of only about half of them, the
half that is making it. There's the other half who have
not gotten on top of things yet. Two men are drunk right
here in the church. One of them's trying to be very self-
controlled and dignified, but he's obviously tipsy, bump-
ing into things. I find myself grinning at him. People in
that state are often fun to watch, like Charlie Chaplin.
The other fellow is bombed, muttering a blue streak to
the empty air beside him. He's actually two people, since

he keeps telling himself he's goddamn right. I think they'll kick his ass out of here, but he dozes off, his chin on his chest.

Several people have faces damaged from years of abuse. You can see it in their skin, all the busted capillaries and the bulges and bags. If their clothes are any indication, it's a cross-section of poor and rich. More farmers than I would have expected, farm work seems to me a bit strenuous for a serious drinker. And young people, a couple of kids can't be over twenty-five. They all know each other and share little jokes that I don't catch. I see that some of them will be no help to me at all. This attractive woman—no more attractive than she thinks she is—says, "When I joined AA, not only did I stop drinking, I also stopped cheating on my husband." I do not want to hear about it. I hope the poor fellow's not here. Maybe he's out drinking somewhere. And I can't stand their endless palaver about "the Man Upstairs." I think of God as Santa Claus for adults, and I wonder how many of these people would be such true believers if they had a job like mine. I read this little blue pamphlet: "Remember that we deal with alcohol—cunning, baffling, powerful! Without help it is too much for us. But there is One who has all power—that One is God. May you find Him now!"

They have a "Twelve Steps" program and you have to say you are "entirely ready to seek God" and "humbly ask Him to remove all your defects of character." No way.

But I like the older people. They seem pretty relaxed, pretty solid. Some of them have been coming for years and years. When I look at this bald-headed guy, Harry, I get these funny stinging sensations all around my eyes, like before tears come. They have "a chip system," a white chip for your first meeting since your last drink, a red chip for ninety days of sobriety, a blue chip for a year and multiples thereof. This one guy gets a blue chip. A night watchman, he's got keys dangling all over him. When a woman gives him his blue chip and hugs him tight, this expression of relief comes over his face like he's made it to heaven. The stinging sensation in my eyes comes again, real strong. I watch the guy jingle back to his chair and sit down, flushed with accomplishment.

One poor old lady says, "This is the only room in the world where nobody has ever lied to me." They tell awful stories about years in institutions, about losing everything, their jobs and their families and finally their self-respect. They owe all they got now to this group. They say if it wasn't for what they found here, they'd be dead. I believe them. I can tell some of my resistance to it is being broken down. Everybody's smoking like crazy. And they laugh a lot. One guy tells about a sober interlude he had. He says, "I was so dry it's a wonder I didn't burst into flames."

When they ask if there are any visitors or anyone here for the first time, I kind of tentatively raise my hand. Dickie's nightmare is very much on my mind. I do what I have heard everybody else do, say your name and then say, "I'm an alcoholic." I'm so accustomed to "Triphammer" that it has become who I am to myself. I have to climb over some years to say my real name, and my voice is not an old man's voice, it's like I am a kid again when I say, "I'm Oliver, and I'm an alcoholic." Everybody says, "Hi, Oliver." Afterward we mill about and put away the chairs and tables. A couple of men come up and shake my hand and give me their phone numbers. They say I should feel free to call at any hour, day or night, and they'll come over if I am having a bad time. Bald-headed Harry gives me a white chip. He says just carry it with your change.

Sydney is waiting for me out in the hall, this hopeful little smile on her face. I don't want to disappoint her. But I don't want to lie to her, either. So in the car on the way home I say, "I didn't have any big revelations. I didn't suddenly feel This Is Where I Belong!" I confess I fought it pretty hard. Sorry. Next week I'll try again. She nestles in real close to me, and we drive the rest of the way home in silence. I continue to have that peculiar stinging sensation in my eyes. In spite of all my efforts not to let this get to me, it has. Jesus Christ, when we pull into the driveway, the stinging has gotten so bad that tears have to come. They run down my cheeks. I have to sit in the car with her for a while.

Dick organizes a poker game for Saturday night at our house. Five guys show up. I sit in for an hour when one boy has to go home to finish his English paper. I can't lose a hand. I don't know why it never happens to me in a real game. I feel like I am stealing little kids' lunch money. I notice this one boy, Duke, real shifty eyes. And something you often hear about but which I had never seen before. Duke is dealing off the bottom of the deck. He's a shitty player, losing heavily, but in this five-card-stud game he is kind of waving the deck around while he is dealing and I see the king of spades on the bottom. The next time around it is the two of diamonds. And then on the last card the king of spades is sitting there part of his hand. Hmmm, I think. I don't mention anything to Dick about it afterward. I figure it is his friend. But then Dick himself mentions it. So we talk. And Dick says Duke has a terrible home life, and he doesn't understand cards too well. Duke probably thinks cheating is just a kind of extreme form of bluffing. I say maybe you should tell him he ought to learn how to cheat *well*. While doing the dishes, we have a little talk about why a gentleman does not check and raise, does not sandbag. Jesus, those boys ate us out of house and home.

I simply cannot accept Dick not going to college. If ever a boy was just obviously fit for it, Dick's that boy. And if he's not going to college, what is he going to do? In a couple of weeks he'll be a high school graduate. Is he going to keep living at home? Does he plan to get a job? He's been getting a lot of mail from military recruiters. Is he going to join the navy and see the world?

Sydney says, "He's got plans."

I say, "What are they?"

She says, "Why not leave him alone till he's ready to talk about them with you?"

I blow up, and I say, "Jesus, don't tease me with it. If you know something, clue me in. I'm his father."

Syd says, "I don't betray confidences."

"So you do know something?"

She clams up.

Which only drives me crazy.

Finally, late one afternoon, Dick sits me down at the dining room table and tells me. I don't even get it at first. He says he's going to Israel for a year to kibbitz. I visualize him sitting beside a card game in the middle of the Sinai peninsula. But it's not kibb*itz* it's kibb*utz*. It's what they call their collective farms. He's going to Israel for a year and live on a collective farm.

If we had played a guessing game, I would not have come up with this in a thousand years. Work on a collective farm? This boy who can hardly mow a lawn? What's it entail? Goat milking? And why? I say, "What meaning does the state of Israel have for you? It is one of the most dangerous places in the whole world. You can't go to a war zone, Dickie. Somebody gets killed over there every day. Where did this crazy idea come from?"

And then the light bulb comes on in my head. Sydney. Who does she think she is? Bad enough that she is plotting with him behind my back about Ala-Teen. But this is serious. It involves his physical safety, his life. I am furious with her. Talk about exceeding your authority. How goddamn dare she? I am weak with fear. At the dining room table I say to Dick, "What's in Israel for you? You're not Jewish."

"Becky is," he says. "Rebecca is Jewish."

Oh.

Well, OK, I got the wrong woman. Rebecca wants Soviet Jews to emigrate, and apparently she wants American Jews to do it too. Dick says, "Her big brother went last year. And he says it was a totally fulfilling experience. It's a lot of work, but he wouldn't have missed it for anything. So Becky's going this year. And I'm going with her."

I see.

I feel guilty and ashamed that I thought it was Sydney. I see her at her locker in seventh grade, and the boys calling her "Jew Dog." I put myself in the circle of boys.

And then I suddenly feel happy. About Dick and Becky. I think it is sweet. I see the two waifs skipping across the burning sand.

And then I see them shot dead by Palestinian terrorists.

Dick says, "The kibbutzim are safe, they're in secure land." He says, "There is this coordinating headquarters in New York. Becky and I have an appointment next weekend. We're going down with her parents."

I need time to think. I cannot fathom it. I can hardly

imagine it. My head is just popping with questions. I say meekly, "You need a passport."

He says, "I've already filled out all the forms."

I try to think of what I can say to deter him. But he'll be eighteen in two months; he'll be "emancipated" from me. I hated that word "emancipated" in the divorce agreement; it made me feel like Simon Legree. But the time has come. This fall he'll be able to vote for president. Though now it looks like he'll need an absentee ballot. It's all just whizzing—whizzing—by me.

I say, "Look, man, give me a while. This is a big deal. I got to get used to it."

He says, "I've given it a lot of thought."

I say, "I'm sure you have. And I'm a hundred percent behind you. I'm just scared about your safety."

He says, "You ought to hear Becky's brother talk about it." He grins at me. "Who knows, Dad? Maybe it'll make a man out of me."

I never thought he'd say anything like that, even in jest. I stare into his gray eyes. I grab his hands across the table. I am holding hands with my son. I say, "You are sure? You are sure this is what you want to do?"

He says, "There's plenty of time for college. When I'm ready for it."

I say, "How about college first, then Israel?"

He shakes his head. He says, "I want it now. With Becky."

I say, "She's a lovely girl."

He says, "She'll read me *Pride and Prejudice* by the Dead Sea."

I say, "I'm sure she will."

Now that I know what's up, he says he'd like me to

share in all their plans. He looks at our hands here on the table. He says he didn't mean to surprise me. He says somehow it had to be a *fait accompli.* He knew I wouldn't go for it, and maybe I'd talk him out of it. He wanted to do it all by himself. He needed to make it definite. Wanted to do a big thing all on his own.

I say I can understand that.

He waits a minute. He sighs. He looks down, and he kind of mutters, "You don't know, Dad. I'm kind of torn between being you and being myself."

"You are?"

"Well, I don't know how to put it. I don't exactly contemplate being a policeman."

"Good," I say, real fast, before I know I've said it.

He says, "I just know I got to do this. I feel in my gut that it's right."

I say, "Then you got to do it. If you know it's right." But I am still flabbergasted. I have to get off by myself.

Which is what I am doing, in my den, wishing I had a glass of Scotch to clarify matters, when Sydney pops her head in. She says, "He told you?"

"Yeah," I say, "thanks for warning me."

She comes in and sits at my feet. She puts her hand on my leg the way she does. She says, "He talked to me about it on the condition that I not tell you. So what could I do?"

I stare at her. I say, "My life has changed completely since you came into it. All sorts of weird things happening. Can't hardly catch my breath from one day to the next."

She says, "Did you like it better before?"

I look out the window at the spring rain. Jesus, my

little boy, way over on the other side of the globe. The trouble with Dickie and me is we got hooked on Jewish women. They lead you astray.

"Well," she says, "did you?"

"Did I what?"

"Like your life better without me?"

"No. Of course I didn't. I can hardly tell you what a stupid question that is."

"He thinks you make all the big decisions. He had to make one."

"Well, he certainly did."

"It's very brave."

Brave? Yes, now that you mention it, I guess it is. I visualize the word. Brave. A right way and a wrong way to live. Brave is the right way to live.

I get up and walk slowly into his room. He's sitting at his desk staring out the window. I approach cautiously and put my hands on his shoulders. We watch it rain. I say, "This life and one more." Mom always said that. Not sure what she meant by it.

Dick says, "You're disappointed in me."

I say, "You got shit for brains if you think that."

There's a little silence.

Sydney comes to the door. She stands there.

Dick says, "Would you guys be at all interested in the International Animation Festival? It's the last night tonight. Cartoons from all over the world, behind the Iron Curtain and everything. Want to go?"

"Sure," I say. "Time I was developing a more international outlook."

Sydney says, "That's true. Whenever the international stories come on the evening news, that's the signal for Trip to go check the vegetables."

Dick laughs. Even I smile. It's true.

We go out into the kitchen and sort of stand around looking for something to do. We bump into each other.

Syd cannot seem to stop smoking. We have talked about it for some time and resolved to quit. She gets bad headaches from it, and a woman who takes contraceptive pills really should not smoke. Myself, I have felt for years this smokey tube in my throat down to my chest, and I know the little tingling in my fingers and toes comes from the way smoking has constricted the blood vessels and resulted in poor circulation. Dick hates the way we stink up the house. So Sydney and I set a date. When it comes, for some reason I find it a breeze. I feel the change immediately. Thirty years of addiction flies right out the window. I have some small nagging discomfort for a couple of days, especially in stress situations on the job, but I am on a roll with my quitting booze. Chuck my bad health habits all at once.

But poor Syd is in agony. She thinks about cigarettes all the time. She'll be watching TV, and I'll look over and her face has an expression like a friend has died. She's been a big smoker for several years; especially when she's writing, she'll fill a big ashtray with butts one right after the other. And this is too much for her. She cheats. Says she forgot something at the Carriage House. But I know what she's up to. She brushes her teeth, but I can smell it in her hair. I say nothing. I am amused. Tickled, actually. Partly because I can do something she can't. One evening she pretends to find an old pack in her coat and says she'll have one for old times' sake. I say, "Don't feel bad, dear. It's not a test of intelligence." Her weakness really surprises her. She thought she could do it and I couldn't. This throws her off stride. She finds something in herself she had not expected.

This is an especially stressful time for her. She has to give a public lecture. Her "diagnostic review" is coming up over at the college; they do it halfway through the contract. This lecture will count pretty heavy for tenure. So she slaves away at her typewriter, in safety at the Carriage House where she can smoke her fool head off. The subject she has chosen is this famous movie, *Citizen Kane*, which we have twice watched together on the VCR. She has studied it for years. Apparently a lot of books have been written about it. "Who can say anything new," she says, "about *Citizen Kane*?" But there's this aspect of it that she thinks she's got a new angle on. She tells me a little about it, and right away I see we are in trouble. It involves politics. And politics is a subject Syd and I hardly ever see eye to eye on. In general, professors are more liberal than policemen. It is very extreme in our case. We've had a couple of bad fights about it. The problem with intellectuals is they love to think about the ills of the world, but they never do anything to change matters. Syd and I had this long argument about what happened in the South when black people got their freedom in the 1960s. Sydney says that when she was a little girl the first concept of a policeman she had was from watching television and the civil rights demonstrators getting beat up by southern policemen turning dogs and

hoses on them. I say to her, Well, who caused that? The
police got blamed for it. But who gives the orders to the
police? Who controls the police? The people in councils,
the people in government. When did you ever see the
mayor of a southern city go on TV and say the police
acted contrary to his wishes? The police are society's
arm, not its head. Police do what the society says it wants
done.

I find it hard to deal with Sydney's arguments because she has all these lofty ideas. I enjoy our talks and
learn from them. But it won't work if she tries to change
me. I know I cannot change her. You can't change an
intellectual. If you change a person, or try, soon that
person becomes resentful, and you have a hell of a mess
on your hands. Opposites attract. Each of us fills a need
in the other. We don't both have to be intellectuals. I've
seen that, and they get divorced all the time.

But it does hurt my feelings when she doesn't come
to me with any problems she runs into with her speech.
I say to myself, Well, she has to work on it over there at
the Carriage House to smoke. But I know it is because
she has given up on my ability to provide any halfway
valuable contribution. When the big day arrives, I swing
by her house to pick her up. I can't believe how she's
dressed. She's got on her mannish Florsheim shoes, and
these speckled soft corduroy pants that are about four
inches too short in the leg, and this baggy blouse. She's a
little defiant, smoking openly.

I say, "I just wonder if that outfit is appropriate, with
all those older people deciding your future."

So she makes a face at me and whips back into her
bedroom and eventually comes out in a better pair of

pants but with cowboy boots and a flashy red shirt and her Star Taxi pin.

I say, "Jesus, that's worse."

Now she gets so flustered she cries. She says, "The way I dress is who I *am*."

I say, "Yeah. And maybe we should talk about that at some future date."

She's blistered, she tears back to her closet again. She shouts, "The idea that I should consult *you* about fashion!"

But I am pretty sure I am right about this. I may not know fashion, but I know a little bit about what's appropriate, especially for the older guys who will be sizing her up. I smile when she comes out in this long white skirt with black polka dots and a pretty blue blouse. Nice string of pearls, the right touch. But she feels defeated, compromised. We drive in 1 GROUCH over to the college, and she smokes, still going over pages with this purple pen, last-minute changes, muttering to herself. She is angry at me. I've rattled her.

It's a big crowd. This auditorium in the performing arts building, lots of students and faculty, it's a hundred people anyway. Syd drops me like I was her driver, and moves along forward through the people, chatting with them. I sit in the back row. It's a noisy bunch, intellectuals jabbering away like monkeys.

The guy who introduces her is this handsome young professor with a tweed jacket that has the customary leather patches on the elbows. He seems to me much more the sort of man she should be living with, so I hate his ass. He praises her teaching and says she has brought new life to the department, and everybody is looking

forward to what she will say, and there will be time at
the end for questions. To a polite smattering of applause
Syd saunters to the lectern in the kind of brash way she
has when she teaches, this nice little flush on her face.
She looks beautiful in the outfit I have forced her to wear.

I pretty much follow the first part of what she says.
I don't feel completely out of my element. She says that
almost everybody associated with the production of *Citizen Kane* was "on the left," and she gives these little
summaries of the people in the Mercury Theater. She
cracks little jokes that make the audience chuckle. She
says that the politics of William Randolph Hearst had
become very right-wing by the time this movie was
made, but in the movie Mr. Thatcher says Charles Foster
Kane "attacked private property—a Communist." The
early crusades of Kane's newspaper, the *Inquirer*, involve
trust busting, copper swindles, and slumlords. Kane's
famous line is "I think it would be fun to run a newspaper," and, Sydney says, "This is left-wing fun." Jedediah
introduces Kane at a political rally as "the fighting liberal," and Kane speaks for "the underpaid, the underpriv-
ileged, and the underfed." After the scandal about his
being trapped in a "love nest," Kane's defeat is said to
"set back the cause of reform for twenty years." Well,
Sydney just bops along through the movie, explaining all
this stuff. She is warm and poised; she steps away from
the lectern and walks around to the front of it and talks
to us conversationally. Everybody is intently listening,
you don't hear any coughing. Syd has the situation well
in hand.

She outlines the other main drive of the movie,
which begins right in the first "News on the March,"

where a street orator calls Kane "a fascist." Syd goes through this other side, and really gets slow and emotional when she quotes old Jedediah again, when he asks Charlie Kane what will happen when "your working man expects something as his right instead of your gift." Maybe Kane isn't a left-wing hero after all. Maybe he's the real William Randolph Hearst. But he doesn't gradually move across the spectrum from left to right; he alternates back and forth. Syd has studied the original scripts, and she goes through some scenes that Orson Welles cut out of the movie, especially this one about Kane's son getting shot when he and a bunch of fascists raid an armory in Washington. I am feeling pretty proud of myself, I can fully understand and would have no trouble if we were given a quiz.

But then I lose her. In what is probably the most original part. It has to do, she says, with "the whole relationship of ideology and art," and she is off and running into theoretical territory. At least it sounds theoretical to me. It's all this stuff about "imaginative assent to the tone and color" of ideas rather than their content. I remember the first time I saw her writing, that afternoon when she had me read the two scenes in *Long Day's Journey into Night* and *Moby-Dick*. When I missed the point. I'm missing it here too. My mind wanders. I size up the crowd, to see the effect she is having. These people, at least, are on her wavelength. You could hear a pin drop. But I start doing dumb stuff, like imagining her up there naked, and that leads me to thinking about how shocked all these people would be if they knew that this highly intelligent woman is spending her life with me, and how shocked they would be if they knew what this professor lady is like in bed. I am ashamed of myself. And what she says about the way we respond to ideas in a work of art is certainly not the way *I* respond. I feel excluded. And I become extremely pessimistic about our future.

I get back on the track a little bit when she draws an analogy to another movie, which we saw together. *A Face in the Crowd.* She says it breaks down into two halves: you love Andy Griffith in the first half and you hate him in the second. But not because Andy changes. It is because the filmmaker's attitude toward him changes. We "respond to his vitality" in the first part, and we don't believe the "smug moralisms about demagogy" in the second. And, she says, when you study the scripts of *Citizen Kane* what really comes out is that Orson Welles loves Charles Foster Kane even more than Herman Mankiewicz scorns William Randolph Hearst. This is the high point of the talk for me. But then she loses me again, and I'm off guard when she finishes. I was wandering away on my own little mental journey. She sure gets a lot of applause.

What pisses me off, more than I can hardly stand, is the first question from the audience. This old broken-down bald professor breaks the silence. Sydney seems to know him, she calls him Jim. Jim says, "Do you think there's any truth to the rumor that Hearst hated the movie because 'Rosebud' was his pet name for Marion Davies' clitoris?"

Jesus. The whole room suddenly goes still as death. Syd looks like she's been slapped. What a question. But Syd makes a little joke of it—she just says in this funny voice, "Not that I know of," and then looks out at us for another question. The audience laughs; they like the way she handled it. But I'd like to get my hands on the old fart. Nothing's sacred to intellectuals, they'll say anything. I steam about it through the next couple of questions.

It's only when the whole thing's over, and everybody's milling about her, that I see what I have been feeling all along. I am so proud. How can such a woman be mine? I watch the young handsome professor kiss her cheek, and I can hardly believe she is going home with the guy who brought her, her fashion consultant.

But she does. And she is bubbling over, flushed with triumph. All the anxiety is gone. In the car when I carry on about how good she was, it seems to mean a lot to her. I say it would just not be possible for me to be prouder of her or to love her more.

She says in this little hushed whispery voice, like a kid, "*Really?*"

I say, "I'd like to wring the neck of that old clitoris guy."

She says, "Well, you know, Skipper, it is the kind of thing Mankiewicz would do. He'd know about it because his wife and Marion Davies spent a lot of time giggling together. Hearst really did hate the movie *so* much. He felt his privacy was invaded. He didn't only want to halt distribution—he wanted the negative burned. Maybe old Jim's right."

She's jabbering on, and when we get inside my house, I stop her by the coat closet and take her in my arms and hug her and kiss her and whisper, "You were *terrific.*" One thing leads to another, and we leave a trail of clothes all the way into the bedroom, and then we are naked except she leaves on the pearls, and we just go crazy with each other, can't get enough, it is all hungry and uncontrollable.

We are very embarrassed when we stumble back out to find Dick seated at the dining room table quietly reading the sports page. We forgot all about Dick. Sydney is especially shamefaced. Did the boy hear us? Syd says she has to go to the Carriage House to pick up some stuff. Which, Dick says to me with a grin, after she's gone, is a cigarette. He knows. I sit here at the table and tell him all about how amazing she was. He leans back in his chair and looks at his father. He sees I am totally in love; his voice is soft and gentle when he says, slowly, "Dad, I think you got a problem." It really brings me up short.

I take Sydney out to the chief's annual Kentucky Derby party. He's had it ever since I can remember, out at his big house in the country. It's always a swell occasion. The whole department is there; the men bring their wives and girlfriends. It starts about four o'clock, and the chief serves these wicked mint juleps. There's a tote board and a lot of betting, everybody gets a little wired. We have a big buffet supper on card tables set up in the dining room and the living room and out on the deck. We play croquet in the twilight, wander about and socialize.

Before, I always got juiced. One year the chief himself had to drive me home. But this time I don't touch the booze. Lo and behold, I have a better time. I enjoy watching Sydney relate to all these half-in-the-bag policemen. She's the prettiest lady there. I kind of show her off. Given her feminist proclivities, we put all our money on the only filly in the race, Winning Colors, and we make a tidy profit. Syd enjoys herself. She goes down to the pond and has this long heart-to-heart with Judy Cook. It surprises me when Judy herself comes up to me on the porch, and says, "Sydney is a lovely person." I just stare. I wonder if we can rehabilitate our friendship again. We have a little talk. Judy is shocked to hear about Dick's

Israel plans. And she is very impressed with my going to AA. She says, "That means you won't die—it gives us twenty more years to fight." All my old deep feelings for her come rushing back.

Sydney and I are the last to leave. The chief takes me aside, on the big gravel driveway, and says, "You better hold on to that girl!" Then he drops his bomb. He says, "Trip, I've been thinking about turning over the reins. I'm not getting any younger. I don't need the constant hassle."

He tells me I am not to breathe a word about this to anybody. I am the senior man. I am next in line. On Monday night the city council is having a closed-door executive session. They want to talk to me. Hear my ideas for the department.

The chief stands here smoking his pipe, rocking on his heels, looking at the moon. He says, "You might try to form in your mind any changes you would make if you could run the show." He says, "Don't get your hopes too high. We'll have to advertise. There is always sentiment that it's better to bring in a man from outside. Instead of promote from within. There'll be well-qualified candidates. But you have good rapport with the men. So far as I know, you got no enemies on the council." He puts his hand on my shoulder. He says, "Triphammer, we have had our disagreements in the past. I was worried about your boozing. More than I told you."

I'm a little uneasy. I wish to hell people had told me. I nod over at Sydney talking with his wife. I say, "Now I got something to stay sober for."

On the drive home I don't tell her about this dramatic turn of events. But she knows me pretty well, she

can tell something's up. She asks me what's on my mind.
I say, "Oh nothing, nothing in particular." But I play with
it and roll it around to myself all day Sunday. I realize
how much I want it. I've dreamed about it, of course.
Never could foresee the day when it would actually
happen. I know I can handle the responsibility. I can
certainly handle the raise in pay. And stupid little things
enter into my mind. Like Sydney has been coaxing me to
go down and meet her parents in New York City. I have
been putting her off. But now I think her father, who I
dread meeting, might look more favorably on this May
and December relationship if I were the chief, not just an
officer. It's a stupid consideration, but I know I will need
every possible plus about myself just to look him in the
eye.

On Monday night I tell Sydney, "It's just a court
appearance—that's why I'm all dressed up."

She says, "Court is Tuesday, Punky, isn't it?"

I say, "This is a different deal."

She's all wrapped up in grading a huge batch of final
papers for school, so she doesn't pay attention. She just
disappears into my den. I go down to city hall, extremely
nervous about what I'll say and what they may ask me.
When I get there, it's just the chief, the mayor, and six
board members, two of them women. The board does a
half hour of bullshit before they come to me. Then they
ask me to come down front, which I do, and I take a
chair. The mayor says this is all off the record, but they'd
like to hear my views. Say I could change three things.
What three things would I change?

I suddenly see the politics of it. I'm in a no-win
situation. There sits the chief, whose recommendation

will carry a lot of weight. And this could be taken as a referendum on his tenure in office. Whatever bright ideas I have will appear as criticism of him. So right away I chuck my main complaint, about the way he handles community relations in general. I toss out all my pre-pared shit about how we got to be part of the community we serve, more than we have been, so that people will turn to police officers instinctively instead of just fearing them. I don't mention my ideas about town meetings and seminars and educating the public. It would look like something he had neglected.

But I do have my other ideas. I say, "The first thing I'd change would be the work shifts. Go to ten-hour work days. Over a long period of time men get burned out. When you have to change over your duty shifts each month—from, say, eleven to seven, to three to eleven—you never get enough break time to reset your clock and adjust your home life. Especially with the extra things we always do, like work holidays and weekends and court time and special time, you don't get the time necessary to get rejunevated." I actually say "rejunevated." I feel so damn ignorant. I stumble over the word twice. But I plunge on. I say, "The advantage would be you'd get four days on and three days off. It would mean working two hours more each day, so you'd still put in a forty-hour week, and I know the men would like it better."

Nobody seems to object to this. But they look at me blankly. Like I just got off the truck. So I say, "The number-two change would be I'd streamline the paper-work. We duplicate too much shit." I catch myself. I actually said "shit." Swell. I begin to sweat under my arms. I say, "I'd make it much easier to do reports of a noncriminal nature. Like dog complaints, and all the public safety stuff we do, potholes and tree limbs down. Ninety percent of that has to be done, and it's important to people. But it does not require long hours at the typewriter. With arrest procedures we could do it in one book, instead of in three or four different places. Computerize things. All tickets, receipts, court dispositions. We could have them so that we could print out the information immediately, have it right at our fingertips. We have not caught up with the times. Most police departments already do this. We're archaic. We certainly could streamline all the DWI work, which now takes about three hours to finish up. I'd make it a standard form, have my man back on the street within the hour. In a small department like ours, if you take a man off the road for an hour, that means the city is unprotected for that hour."

This they like better. A flicker of interest in their eyes. I also know the chief has been pushing for this, and he's nodding and smiling at me. So I kind of warm to my subject. I'm listening to my voice, which as Sydney says is the sexiest thing about me. But this isn't for Most Sexy, this is for Chief. I say, "The third main change I'd institute would be an optional twenty-year retirement plan. Anybody who puts in his twenty years would be able to retire at half pay. I think it is terrible to be trapped in this job, given the stress of it. I am myself going into my twenty-third year now, and I am just not physically able to do the things I did as a rookie. I get hurt all the time."

I look at the board members, especially the two women. I say, "Would you want your son to be a policeman? No, you wouldn't. My own boy, Dick, is about to graduate from high school. A fine boy. Just the other day we were talking about what he will do with his life. Would I want him to be a policeman? No. Not at all. A rookie starts out now at pitiful pay. Really pitiful. How can we hope to attract bright young people? How can you expect to get first-class service out of your police department if you don't make the job attractive from a financial standpoint?"

I stop. I've said that part OK. Now what? "Very few people want to do this job to begin with. It's a lousy job in some respects, a dirty job. You clean up dead people, you deal with things society cannot cope with, or does not want to. If you are going to be the garbage man of society, then society should at least pay you a decent wage as a sign that they respect you and need you. Most people could not put up with the stress and strain and aggravation of this job. Policemen are human beings and they give up a lot of their lives to serve their communities. We get very little in return."

Now I'm cooking. I've got their full attention. I thought I could do this. I spoke at Rotary once, on the subject of handguns. "Usually you make very few friends—you have to give up on that aspect of life. A wide circle of friends is not compatible with the job. If you are an elite cabinetmaker, a person will pay you top dollar or he doesn't get his cabinet. Here, the system we work under now is pretty demeaning. We are not allowed to go out on strike. The law prohibits it. Imagine if all the policemen were to walk off the job and leave this city to police itself. Things would be in total chaos within a week. Look at the pittances we get for raises. When the governor gets ten percent, it's ten percent of ninety thousand dollars. And we have to fight like a bastard to get seven hundred fifty dollars. We barely keep up with the cost of living. I think it's time this country straightened up and put their policemen in the proper perspective. If we do not perform our job to your satisfaction, get rid of us. If we do do the job right, give us adequate compensation and recognition. Excuse me if I am mounting a soapbox. But I feel deeply about these matters, and I have thought about them for some time."

Well, they look at me as though their dog talked. I know I have made a strong impression. I just don't know if it's a good one. I realize these are the people you have to hammer out a budget with. Maybe they won't want a hard-liner who will scratch and claw for every penny. But at least I have been frank and aboveboard.

The chief says, "Well, now you can see why I am enthusiastic about this guy." He says, "Does anybody have any questions?"

There is a silence, for a long time. It seems to me a negative sign. I can't read the thing. Maybe it's just a charade, maybe they've already got an outside candidate. It wouldn't be the first time in my life I thought I was on top of something and then found out it was all put together a different way. Like with Sheila.

One of the women board members says, "What about rubber gloves?"

I have to think a minute. I stall for time. Finally I say, "People don't realize the risk you take every time you touch somebody. How does the public want a policeman to respond? If you wear rubber gloves all the time, it's like you're in a leper colony or back in Colonial days when you feared to get near somebody because they had whooping cough. I would turn the question back around to you and ask what society wants done. A policeman is in a quandary. How do you fingerprint someone without touching them? In most jobs you don't touch people. Doctors do, but they've got all sorts of protection, like gowns and masks and gloves. I'm not a doctor. I don't work in a antiseptic environment. When we got a traffic accident, do you disinfect the car? You don't know what illnesses people have. They don't wear a little sign. Often you've got three or four bodies jammed in there, and one of them could have AIDS. There's metal and broken glass—you reach in to help someone and you very likely cut yourself, and there's blood all over the place. Do you wear rubber gloves to the scene of everything? You have to act fast, sometimes a life hangs in the balance. You look pretty foolish if you drive up to the scene of an accident where people are screaming and unconscious, and you get out of the cruiser, and go back and open the trunk, and put on your rubber gloves, and close the trunk, and then walk over to the wreck. I don't really know. It's a concern of young officers. 'Am I going to die of infection before I finish my twenty-year career? Do I put my wife at risk of a deadly disease?' "

They ask me a few more questions, which I field to the best of my ability. I kind of relax and just talk with them honestly. Then I am excused. I go out and pace in the hall. I wait around, but they go on with their executive session. Finally I just go home. I am a little withdrawn. Sydney probably thinks I am having a rough time with the booze. But I'm not. I hardly think of it. I just go over all that I meant to say and didn't. I think of all the things I actually did say and should not have. I don't sleep well, I toss and turn.

I can't get a bead on it until the next morning when the chief calls me in and says, "Triphammer, you done good." He seems to mean it. He says the council was impressed with my sincerity. Not, I note, my intelligence or ability. Any darn fool can be sincere. But the chief gets kind of mellow. He says, "It is going to be a shock to my system when I retire." He says, "I remember something that the distinguished journalist Theodore White once said." He actually puts it that way. He says, "White was interviewing Eisenhower in the Oval Office during his last month in office. Kennedy had beat Nixon in November. Ike sighed and said to White, 'Somehow I always pictured Dick at this desk.' " I look at the chief, and he says, "Somehow, Trip, I have always pictured you at this desk."

Swell. I'm Richard Nixon. I'm the guy who lost.

But the chief is ever the chief. He says, "You are a little rough around the edges, as was I when I assumed command. But you are a more thoughtful person as you mature. I've noticed a big change just in the past year."

My teeth itch. I wonder what will happen. But if I don't do something stupid, and keep my wits about me, I think I have the inside track.

He says, "It will be decided before the snow flies."

Jesus, before the snow flies.

I have a devil of a time not telling Sydney. But she is all wrapped up in grading those term papers. I admire the huge amount of time she puts in. She fills up their margins with her comments. Spends a good hour on each one. She doesn't have to; she just feels it is her job and she must do it to the best of her ability. I poke about and look in on her and realize how much I adore her. We are going to have to do something about it. Of course we could just go on like this. No point in fixing something that's not broke. I wish I could solve the difference in our ages. That really worries me. There's no way I can get around it. What do you do when you totally love a woman but think your love may not be in her best interest? It might not catch up with us for ten years. But it certainly will in twenty. When she's middle-aged, I will be an old man. She will want to do all sorts of things that I have lost interest in. If I truly love her, I will not put her in that position. But I do truly love her and cannot imagine life without her. No question she's changed me. Permanently. How can you not love someone who does that to you and for you?

On Father's Day she has a bright idea. We should go fishing. This does not appeal to me. I have never caught a fish in my life. When I was a little boy, my stepfather liked to fish, but I'd never last an hour standing out in the middle of the river with him. Too boring. I'd quit and go back to the car and play gin rummy with my mother. But for some time now Sydney has wanted us to see the farmhouse where she lived her first year here. So we pick up Becky and go. It's miles from town, way the hell out in rural poverty, this big old ramshackle house full of flies. It's hard for me to picture a City Girl here. She says that was the appeal. So we load ourselves down with camp chairs and buckets and rods and reels and beach towels. We hike and hike through this meadow with itchy grass up waist-high, and finally we come to this huge pond. It's a gorgeous afternoon, hot as hell, and we set up camp in the middle of a bed of wildflowers. We're all in our swimsuits, Sydney in this black bikini that hardly covers a thing and Becky in a tank suit. We are also all wearing old shitty sneakers, which Syd told us to, because the bottom is full of rocks and squishy mud and you have to walk out almost to the middle before it's deep enough to swim. The kids splash around, and the old folks go ashore to fight the bugs. Sydney's brought along the *New York Times*, and she peruses the fashion section while I plough through sports. If the kids could go over behind a little island, they could skinny-dip modestly there, and Syd and I could flash about over here. It's so goddamn hot I got a boner. Which I cover with the *Times* when the kids come back. Dick's eager to catch a fish. So Sydney takes him out into the water and shows him how to work the gear. She seems to know what she's doing. He's a bit of a fumbler, but he catches on, and Syd splashes back, splattered with mud in that black bikini. I'm horny as hell and try to think up excuses for her and me to disappear into the woods.

Dick actually hooks a fish. He lets out a shout, and we yell encouragement, and he struggles and plays it and eventually lands it in his little net. He rushes back to show us, and it's good size. We throw it in a bucket. Sydney says it's a bass. Dick hustles on back out into the water, he's got the bug now. We watch him, he looks so manly to me, my little boy, tall and strong and in great shape. I understand what Becky sees in him. I am still extremely worried about their going to Israel. I dread the departure day.

But before I can get too down in the mouth, Dick catches another fish. This is not at all like it was with my stepfather. It seems all you have to do is drop your line in. Sydney says it's feeding time, they'll go for anything. So I say I'll give it a try. There's a first time for everything. I get a rod and reel and my son teaches me the way Sydney taught him. We stand out here thigh-deep, and he says, "It's in the wrist."

I say, "It usually is." I am pretty clumsy. Then I see how it works, and I actually have fun letting the line zing way out there and go *plop* in the water. I get to enjoy myself. Dick is all smiles.

Nothing much happens for several minutes, and my attention begins to wander. Then I get a strike, a good big hard one, and the sucker runs with it. I about piss my pants in the water. My fishing pole bends double. I can't believe it. I'm shouting, and Dick is also shouting—he cries, "Don't lose him—don't lose him"—and I am frantically thinking, Are you kidding? I won't lose him.

My fish jumps up and wiggle-waggles in the sunlight. I even think I see his eye look at me, the Stone Age eye of my fish. I got him hooked in his jaw, and he jumps again, and goes *flappity-flap*, and it is just tremendously exciting. On shore Sydney is shouting "Oh" or "Go" or something. I probably do it all wrong, but I am frantically reeling him in, as he goes tug-tug. Dick comes to my side with the little net, and we put him in. He's huge. I go *slop-slop* on the squishy bottom back toward dry land. I lose my footing and kind of squat down, holding high the rod and the net, and kind of sway around.

Dick shouts to the sky, *"Father and son fishing!"* and he laughs and sits down in the water. I have caught a *fish!* at my advanced age. He's flapping around in there to beat the band; he's a fighter. Sydney comes, helps me up, and Dick comes *splashity-splash* out to join us. God, my fish is humongous, over a foot long. When I try to get the hook out of his mouth, the son of a bitch bites me with his razor-sharp teeth. Blood spurts from my thumb, it doesn't really hurt, and Dick smears the blood on his fingers and then he paints a little cross on my chest between my nipples, like this is an ancient Indian rite.

Well. I am King Shit. I am tickled pink. I don't want to try again—I'll never top this. I get a bit annoyed with Sydney, who first decides it's a pike, which sounds great to me, but after a while she thinks maybe it's a pickerel, which I don't like nearly as much because it sounds small. I say it's a pike, goddamn it, a man-eater, not a little pickerel. I go into a song and dance about how ferocious my fish is. I say my fish and I were out there, we were dick to dick, and the fish blinked. It was a heroic battle, like *The Old Man and the Sea.* Which I have not yet read. I turn to my son, I am just kidding and he knows it, but I am also doing it for Becky's benefit, just to get her dander up. I say to Dick that you can catch those feminine bass, but I got a phallic pike, my fish is male, and hard and lean and long, and your fish is female and heavy and round and plump and no teeth.

Sydney says, "Oh, you are Trouble-Hook Triphammer. The fish are all hiding on the bottom now—they're afraid of ol' Trouble-Hook." Except I wonder if she said

"Treble-Hook." I hear her say we ought to "flay" them,
which, after she says it again, I realize she has said
"fillet" them. My hearing is going, along with my butt.
But I caught my fish!

Old Mrs. Nordland has led me a merry chase for years. She's a tiny person, barely five foot, and whenever she takes off on one of her little expeditions, she speaks French. Every month or so she'll get the itch to take a hike, and she ends up here and there—you'll find her someplace like in the backseat of a rent-a-car in the parking lot at the Sheraton Inn. People don't know what to do with this elderly lady and her *parlez-vous*. I call her Our Wanderer.

She wasn't so bad when her husband was alive, Ole Nordland, a supreme court judge. Their stately old house must have ten bedrooms. All this oak paneling, deep white carpets, everything plush. They used goldware, not silverware. Outside, all the shrubs trimmed to perfection. It's probably the most beautiful home in town, sitting so majestic on three or four lots, with rock gardens and walkways and statuary. They've got this temple to Diana and other such oddities. Peacocks strutting about. One time back there when Ole was alive, I got this call on a Sunday afternoon from a college student who said he found a peacock in the backyard of this house where he rented a room, about a mile away from the Nordland mansion. How many people in town keep peacocks? So I drive down to the Nordlands, hit the intercom, and she comes to the door. I ask her if she's missing a peacock. She says yes, one's been gone about a week, why? I say this kid found it, and I tell her where he lives. She says she and Ole will go get it. About an hour later I see them in one of their many cars—this one's a big old fifties Cadillac, mint condition, which starts by remote control. It had previously been a gangster's car, and the idea was to be able to start it from two blocks away in case somebody booby-trapped it. So here they come—she's driving and Ole's beside her with a big butterfly net. I forgot about them until some time later when I was back at the station. A car pulls up with its horn blasting away like it's stuck, and she's driving and Ole's got this huge peacock jumping around in the backseat. Ole can't manage it at all—peacock shit flying.

But after Ole died, she began to falter. One night about 2:00 A.M. I get a call, there's an air-horn blowing at the Nordlands'. I go and knock and knock, but who can hear me when this deafening huge *beeeep beeeep* is going, just like a tractor-trailer is in the house. I finally get in, and she is upstairs in one of the bedrooms. I wonder if this is some kind of super smoke alarm. The horn finally stops, and I identify myself to her, and she unbolts the door. She has used up this air canister they gave her at a senior citizens' meeting. She says she heard footsteps. So I look around. Nothing. No footprints in the dewy grass. Which makes me suspicious the next time she calls, saying naked children are running around in her yard. I sigh and think, What next? But I go down there, and when I pull in, I see that she's right. There are a dozen kids in various states of undress, eleven to thirteen years old. I am able to round up four or five of them and gather their clothes. It was a birthday party, and they played spin the bottle. Only instead of getting kisses like we used to do, every time the bottle points at you you got to take off an article of clothing. Some of the kids were standing around nude behind trees. I called the parents, who were not too happy. I rather enjoyed it, seeing all the little bare asses going every which way.

Once in the dead of night she calls to say she has an intruder in the attic. I figure it's possible. She's a very inviting target, a wealthy old woman living alone. It's raining and lightning, a nasty night, and I go upstairs with my flashlight in one hand and my radio in my back pocket turned down low. I'm way up there in the attic, a bit jittery from all the cobwebs and the thunderclaps outside and the lightning. The attic door is ajar, and it does sound like a person brushing against something. I step in. It is partially floored; the rest is just insulation lying flat. I sweep with the flashlight, right to left and back, waiting for the person to come out at me. There's a big chimney right in the center—a person could be hiding behind it, it's wide enough. I really don't want to walk out on the rafters, because if we have a confrontation, we'll likely end up down on the third floor, go right through the ceiling and land in a bedroom. I stand on my plank, and then I see him, a big ball of fur, a raccoon. The little peckerhead's got his hands up like he's saying, "Don't shoot!"

She complains of vandalism. She shows me her flower beds, or what once were flower beds and now are just weeds. She says, "The neighborhood children run through my flower beds." I think of the old spin-the-bottle fracas, so I check with the neighbor kids. They deny it. They say she is too strange now, they stay away except to deliver the paper. And when they come to collect, she says she already paid. She's in her nineties. She calls in all the time about terrible things being done to her property. But it is just slowly deteriorating for lack of proper care. She has become a recluse. Eats mostly out of tunafish cans and bags of peanuts. The once noble house has become dirty inside. One bitter wintry night she calls, and I go down there at 1:00 A.M. It was terrible cold in there—she kept it around fifty. Even though she has plenty of money, she has become very frugal and paranoid. The house was so cold it was no wonder she got sick and had to be put in the hospital for a couple of weeks.

I call her daughter in California and say you got to make arrangements for your mother. But nothing gets done. This spring Our Wanderer calls me to say somebody is scraping paint off the house. It's a lovely warm day, bright sunshine, but she has on a sweater and heavy coat, all bundled up, with long wrinkly socks all fallen down around her ankles. Now she is so eccentric she wears strange costumes. Her fingernails like talons. This wealthy lady wears her fine jewelry, and I am afraid she will lose it somewhere. In the lovely sunshine she takes me around to the back of the house, where the weeds grow up past your ankles. She shows me where vandals have been throwing paint thinner on the house. But it's just weathering. She is sticking by her story, though, and she says, "The children throw fluid on it to make it peel." So I figure she's really starting to lose it. I suggest that we go sit on the porch and talk about this. She seems to be tickled that I will sit and talk with her for a few minutes. I figure that's all she wants anyway, just someone to talk to. After a bit she says, "You know something? The children in this neighborhood are not natural."

I say, "What do you mean they're not natural?"

"Well," she says, "they turn into birds. We have to be very quiet while we're talking here. You see those two crows up there? That's the boy and the girl, and they're watching us."

I look at her and I think, Yeah. I say, "What makes you think they turn into birds?"

"Oh," she says, "at night when it's dark and quiet and black and no moon, a taxicab pulls up into the driveway. The children get out. There are always six or eight of them. They walk through the backyard. Lights come up out of the ground and light a path. One night I followed them. They were selling popcorn and showing the other children movies. When the movies are over, the lights come back up out of the ground and light a path back over to the taxicab."

I am watching her and thinking, Oh boy, she's really gone whacky. But she is very insistent. We have to speak low because of the crows. They fly around at night and do bad things to the house. Lately they have begun stealing trees. I already told Judy Cook to call me down here in about half an hour, with a fictitious call, so that I can leave without being offensive. Mrs. Nordland says, "I had five pine trees in my yard, and now there are only two left."

I say, "What do you mean there are only two left?" I'm looking out there at them, and there are five pine trees.

She says, "Well, there were other trees in between

them. These are sixty feet tall and the others were only half that tall. The garbage crews have taken them."

I say, "How could they take them without leaving some kind of hole where the tree was?"

She says, "They covered over the holes with grass. I want the city engineer to come."

Who actually does come is the daughter. For a week. And Mrs. Nordland is able to put on an act of rationality. But as soon as the daughter returns to California, her mother starts calling us again. Parker goes down, and he has no patience, and he tells her if she keeps bothering us, we'll have to arrest her. So a few days later I hear the siren at the firehouse, and I follow and discover that she was afraid to call us, so she called the fire department. Her neighbor is barbecuing. There are five trucks down there, and now the fire chief gets all mad at her. So she starts calling us again.

I get hold of the daughter in California again. I say, "Please come take care of your mother. Your mother is not gathering it together in one basket. She needs to be evaluated, or go out to California and live with you. At least get her a nurse so she can eat well."

The upshot is that the daughter hires this guy to live in. Leon, a heavy drinker—he was fired from the postal service. He's got this droopy handlebar moustache. A big fella, but not entirely stable. Mrs. Nordland supplies him with money, clothing, and food. He mows her lawn and takes care of the property and drives her everywhere. Things look okay. At Christmas she has a little party for us, cookies and sweet wine. I hope she can live out her remaining time in relative peace.

But this group of three or four teenagers appears on

the scene. They begin hanging around. They take her out
to their spots, and she seems to have a swell time. The
problem is Leon. He gets jealous when two of the kids
virtually move in. She's enjoying getting out of the house
and going places. Leon feels displaced, and so he threat-
ens the kids. He tries to outdo them and get back in her
good graces. His personality changes. Before, he was very
cooperative, but now he tends to shun us. Lots of things,
valuables, begin disappearing from the house. Probably
it's the kids, selling them to buy drugs. Leon locks the
kids out. The whole thing begins to look ominous. A
volcano building up. But no laws have been broken, so we
cannot intervene. I don't really follow all the ins and outs
and details of what is going on, but I am afraid for Our
Wanderer. Her eyes are sunk way back into her little
head. She's such a sweet little old lady, half in the other
world anyhow, and my hopes for a peaceful conclusion
are dim. There's too much commotion in the old house.
Too many kids, too much Leon. He gets pretty rough
with one of the kids. I think maybe I could lay a reckless
endangerment on him.

One night in June, very late, I am up to my ears in
our useless paperwork. I'm typing my twenty words a
minute, swearing at all my errors, and this teenager
comes in huffing and puffing, all agitated. He says, "Leon
has taken everybody hostage in a back bedroom. He's got
a gun. He says he's going to shoot them."

I'm all alone at my post. There's been a serious
accident out on Route 13, and both the other night
officers are all involved there. I haul my ass straight down
to Nordland's, dreading the worst, as you always do.

The house is all dark, locked up tight as a drum. But

I remember this little door way down in the basement, a rickety door barred by an old hand-push mower that's all rusted. The lock on that door seems to be secure, but in reality it's not. I put my shoulder to it and it pops right open. I creep upstairs through the darkness, which is pitch black, unrelieved by moonlight. Leon has all the blinds down and the drapes pulled. A shot rings out. It's a huge old house, like a haunted mansion. The shot came from the upper floors. I stealthily go up. Nobody on two. On three I check the bedrooms. Down at the end of the hall I see a crack of light underneath a door. I go there and call out who I am. I say, "Leon, open the door and let the kids out."

He says, "They're all out." He says, "It's just me and the old woman."

I say, "Well, let her out, Leon."

He says, "She can't come out. She's dead."

This news gets me very upset. I say, "Maybe she's just fainted."

He says, "No, she is dead." He sounds drunk. He says, "Go away or I'll start hurtin' people."

I say, "Who can you hurt, Leon, if the kids are out and Mrs. Nordland is dead?"

I hear him dial the telephone and talk and hang up. I wonder if I should kick the door down and take him. I try the door. To my total surprise it is unlocked. I gently push it open. I shine my flashlight to the hinge side on the back of the door to see if he is behind it, hiding and waiting for me to come in. This time the light hits these two feet, shoes and trousers. I've done it a thousand times and never once saw anything. Now, when I do, I am flabbergasted that he's really there. I go in, very wary. I kind of sidle back away from the door, and he comes out into view. He's got both his hands behind his back. I know he's hiding something. He says, "Get out of here." He's as big as I am. That stupid droopy moustache.

I say, "We are going to talk this situation over."

"Fuck you," he says, "get out!"

He just stares at me. He's drunk. He takes a step closer; he's about six feet from me. My eyes are jumping from him around the room. Suddenly I see Mrs. Nordland lying there on the bed, her nightie pulled up. She's got dried excrement all caked on her spindly little legs. She's dead all right. Her face all twisted up. In the blur I get of it, she looks like she's in terrible pain. She also looks like she is embarrassed to have soiled herself. My eyes are whipping back and forth between him and her. I'm braced for action, but I'm kind of all wilted inside by the shock of Our Wanderer being gone. I have this split-second flash of my mom at the end.

I am not really frightened. More catlike. My senses have become very alert. I know that I may have to do something fast. I wonder what the hell he's hiding behind his back. Which is why I do not move in on him. It may be a gun. I realize that I have no vest on, and that would be fitting, that would be dandy—I would not wear my vest on just the night when I get my ass blown away. He may have nothing at all in his hands, and I don't want to be the one who shoots him for no reason. My fear instinct starts to take over, and I really am puzzled as to why he stands there like that with his hands behind his back. I know I got no backup coming. If this gets to be a wrestling match, it is going to be just me and him. I got to hurt him right off the bat so that I don't get winded.

I say, "I am going to have to arrest you, Leon."

And then he pulls out his hands from behind his back. What he has been hiding from me is a long butcher knife. It is only about ten or twelve inches long, but it looks like a sword. I take a couple of steps backward. I say to myself unconsciously, Draw your weapon, you dumb ass. But my hands won't do anything. I say out loud, "Leon, things are going from bad to worse."

He waves that butcher knife at me. He tells me to get out of the house.

I say, "No, Leon, you are going out of this house, one way or another." I really wish I had someone here with me, so as we could section him off. Finally, I do get my weapon out. I point it at him and I say, "Look, pal, the time has come that we are all done talking."

Leon looks at me for a long time as if he is not quite able to comprehend that it is actually a gun pointed at him. He just stares at me with those blank drunken eyes. I am thinking, Where do I shoot him? Do I just shoot his arm? Do I shoot him in the leg or shoot over his head to scare him? I say, "If you do not put down the knife, Leon, I am going to blow your ass away." I am almost within arm's length of him, and he could stab me. It bothers me to have my gun out; my hands are shaking, and I could shoot the bastard accidentally. I say, "Look, Leon, you come one step closer and I really am going to shoot you."

He says, "Fuck you, you have no business here, get out."

I have this kind of death-smell in my nose. Maybe it's because there is a body in the room, but it is more like a premonition, this sinking feeling I have that this is my last night on earth. I am smelling my own death. All weak and trembly, I cock my gun. I say, very slowly, "You asshole, put that fucking knife down or I am going to blow you away." I figure this is it. I am going to dust him. There is no question in my mind. One step closer, motherfucker. I am afraid he will lunge and get me. I have my cocked gun pointed right between his eyes. I draw the gun back to me a bit. I'll shoot him in the head, and that'll blow him backward. I got to protect myself.

I can hear every sound. I hear Leon breathing, and I even hear me breathing. We stand here without moving for a full minute. It seems like an hour. Then Leon takes this little half-step backward and bows his head. I think it's over. I start to holster the gun. I am thinking, Now we can sit down, talk matters over. And without warning the son of a bitch lunges at me. Do I shoot him? Like I had 100 percent planned to do? No. I get my gun back up, just whip it up, but then I do the weirdest thing I have ever done: my gun is like a hot potato—I kind of half throw it and half let go of it, and it jumps straight up into the air. It seems to just hang there. Leon is so fucking startled he misses me. I turn and kick his legs out from under him, and the butcher knife sails and clatters across the bare floor. Leon goes down hard. And then I am jumping up and down on him, kicking and stamping like I can kill him with my feet. I guess I am shouting because I sure the fuck can hear it.

I can't exactly say what society should do with Leon. It's an interesting question. My first answer would be to do to him what I didn't do to him when I had the chance. I think we can safely say he is guilty of resisting arrest. He is guilty of all sorts of diddly-shit minor charges. And he will pay for them. But that's not enough. To leave it at that seems to me to dishonor Mrs. Nordland. In some sense he killed her. But good luck proving it in a court of law. She was ninety-three. She should have been in a hospital, but Leon couldn't force her to go. He was not legally responsible for her. So you can't even really charge him with neglect.

A discovery we made was that he had persuaded her to put him in her will. He stood to benefit from her passing on. But I'm not an executioner. I'm not even a judge. I'm a policeman. It is not my job to mete out punishment. So I did the right thing. If you can call tossing your gun in the air the right thing.

Mrs. Nordland had been dead for some time, and Leon just locked himself in there with her body. Who knows what he may have to say in his own defense?

Whole thing hits me pretty hard. It is a wonder I don't fall off the wagon. In my former days there would have been no question about it, something like this

would guarantee a trip to the liquor store. But after I
booked Leon down at the jail, I came home to find
everything peaceful and still. Dick and Sydney asleep. I
tried to be very quiet. I knew I couldn't sleep yet, so I
made myself a cup of coffee, instead of a glass of Scotch.
I sat there at the dining room table drinking it. Then this
very interesting thing happened. I didn't hear her get out
of bed—I didn't know quite where she had come from.
But all of a sudden while I was sitting there at the table
with the whole evening's events churning around inside
me, I felt this pair of soft arms around my neck. I don't
know, that drowsy hug of hers made me feel safe. Warm
and human again. We sat there and talked for an hour.
Maybe an hour and a half. I could feel all the fear and
upset just leaving me. She was removing it, taking out
the pieces one by one. I don't know how she did it.
Sydney is a very smart lady. She seems to have developed
a knack for it.

Ordinarily I never let anyone in the deep part of my
life. I do not tell Sydney a lot of things that happen on
the job. There is no sense in upsetting her and getting
her worried so that she is afraid all the time about
whether or not someday there will be a knock at the door
and a man will be standing there waiting to tell her I'm
dead. I do not dwell on the hazards. Sometimes it will be
days later when she will read something in the newspaper and say, Jesus, honey, were you involved in this thing
over at such and such a place? I say yeah—you know, no
big deal. But you have to be careful of that, you do not
want to haul too much baggage around. It is like you are
a porter carrying all these suitcases. When you load
yourself with more of them than you can handle, you are

going to drop one eventually. Then you have got yourself
in big trouble. You manage the suitcases you can. But
once in a while you have to ask somebody to help you
with one. So you can be a healthier person. There is only
a certain amount you can do anyway. You handle an
immediate situation, get a person into the right avenues
of help, and move on. If you get too emotionally involved,
you get yourself hurt. You can't overload your system.
You cannot think the world's problems are yours.

We have guys who quit the force all the time; they
go into something less stressful, like the Welfare Fraud
Division or private security systems, where they guard
an empty building and walk around all the time and do
not have to answer emergencies. Emergencies are what
do it to you. On television, cops are always working on
"cases." There is a whole long plot. Developments. Sur-
prising twists and turns. But that is false. That is not
what this job is. In reality, it is one thing after another.
Disconnected. You never know when you will have to
risk your life. And not get paid for it. Dentists earn
considerably more than police officers. How many dentists are killed in the act of filling a tooth? On this job
you think all the time, not about lofty ideas, sometimes
just about getting hurt. You can be riding around just
writing tickets, and then all of a sudden you are ass-deep
in blood and guts. You are expected to know all the
answers. You move from being clergy to paramedic to
nurse to psychiatric social worker, and you are expected
to handle it all. You pretend you can do it. But you can't.

There has developed this strange code that you are
some kind of sissy if you show emotion. I don't know
where all this crap started that a policeman has to be a

stone-face. You arrive at the scene of an accident and a little kid has a Coke bottle jammed down his throat. You see people with their bones sticking out or their heads gone. Nobody can really deal with it. How do you go home? How do they expect you to put a lid on your feelings and write this down, and write that down, and have it all at your fingertips? What you write down back at the office are things in chronological order. But you do not insert your own personal feelings. If you show emotion, you are said to be out of control. But you can be emotional and not be out of control. You go into the house of an old couple that has been married for sixty years, and the husband has died and the wife is sitting there on the floor with this dead man's head in her lap and stroking his eyebrows and talking to him. How can you see that and not feel sadness? It is sad. It changes you. The rule of thumb is not to bring your work home. And it is a good rule. But you can't just tell your troubles to a bottle. You need someone who loves you. When you tell, when you are heard the way you need to be heard, it lets you see yourself from the outside instead of having it pile up inside you. When you come home you have to be able to take off the uniform. Lay your police clothes away.

After Sydney and I got into bed, I could tell that she was thinking about what I had told her. She was mulling it over in the dark beside me. And she picked up on a little detail in my story: when I saw Our Wanderer, I had that brief flash of my mom at the end of her life. Sydney says that I have never really told her very much about the time my mom died. I don't tell her now. I do not tell her—and will never tell anybody—that I actually assisted my mother to die. But lying here in bed, I remember the helplessness I felt when I was watching my mother suffer and there was no hope of recovery. I stood there at the foot of Mom's bed, and I thought of all the scumbags I had saved, that I didn't even know. I had revived them, given them oxygen, pulled them out of wrecks. But here I stood helpless to save my own mother. It was an awful feeling. And after she died, I had to organize the funeral and call all the people. I never had time to cry. Back then I believed the macho shit about how real men never cry. I put the shield up, this bullet-proof, emotion-proof shield. You just push a button on your belt, and it slides up in front of your face, and any and all emotions bounce off. In bed, Syd's body all nestled close to me, she said this real simple thing. She said, "You know, it's okay to cry." I don't understand how such a simple statement could trigger it. I guess it was her voice, and the way she was holding me. And I cried. And then we made love, all slow. Next morning I felt like this huge weight had been taken off me. I had let all my feelings go. Syd has me figured out. She could hear me calling her to come get me.

Graduation week at the high school

is full of brunches and open houses. We go to them all. I observe little glances between husbands and wives as they watch me and Sydney together, Father Christmas and his cutie-pie. We've got to meet Becky's parents, since our children are having this great adventure together. We share a table at an outside buffet supper. It's windy; things blow away and fall over and spill. I guess Becky gets her looks from her dad and her brains from her mother. It's clear who wears the pants in the family. The mother is homely as a mud fence, way overweight. You'd think with two incomes she could afford a comb. She's the chairperson of the sociology department at the college. She's pissed at a chairman out in Indiana somewhere. He wrote this recommendation letter for a young woman applying for an assistant professor job here. Becky's mother has memorized a sentence: " 'Miss Charters is a lesbian, I believe, but since she is a young woman of great charm and discretion, it is no one's business but her own.' " I see the point. I go tsk-tsk. I also think it's kind of funny. I see the poor fool writing it, getting all balled up. But I agree with Becky's mother that the old-boy network has got to go. Thinking silently to myself, I hope it holds on until I get to be chief. The cat is out of

225

the bag at the station now, and I am a little disappointed when a couple of the men hang around me, sucking up to me. They know I got the inside track. I play it cool. I pretend not to want the job. You are always much more attractive if they think you have other plans.

Becky's father teaches physics in junior high. He says to me, "That son of yours is such a life-affirming individual." Give me a break. We have a debate on capital punishment. He says, "It brings out the animal in us. It makes us a little more bloodthirsty than we need to be." I totally disagree. But I mind my manners.

Becky and Dick are inseparable. Are they virgins? I bring it up to Sydney at home. She laughs and says, "Oh, Scooter, they've been sleeping together for a year and a half." Which once again shows how firmly I got hold of things—I don't miss a trick. But I am proud of my son, that he keeps it so private. I used to love him to pieces, but now I'm getting rather fond of him.

I am not too fond of him on the big day when Romeo and Juliet Go to the Middle East. We've all been out doing last-minute errands. When I pull into the driveway at noon, his Chevy is sitting there with the whole rear end bashed in. It's a wonder he was able to drive it home. I'll bet it's at least a thousand bucks this time. I go into the house where he and Sydney are packing him up for the long journey, and he doesn't even mention it. I wait around and finally I say, "What the hell happened to your car?"

He says, "It wasn't my fault, I was just sitting there at a stop sign. And this old couple from Canada rear-ended me. The man said he was a stranger in town and never even saw the stop sign." But Dick has not taken down their insurance information, all he knows is they're staying at the Sheraton.

I say, "What is to keep this couple from slipping back across the border and sticking you, meaning me, with the bill?"

Dick turns sullen.

I go into my den.

Eventually he pokes his head in and says, "I just didn't think. I'm all distracted by this trip."

I am thinking, You remember how you always used to ask me what's wrong with not growing up? It's because then you are a perpetual child. You are always asking people to clean up the messes you make. Like a widdle kid. I don't say it, but I'm kind of ashamed of myself for even thinking it. We only have about two hours left. I don't want him to go halfway around the world with a bad taste in his mouth. So I say, "I'll take care of it. I'll try to get hold of the Canadians. Was there a police officer at the scene, or did you just ride off into the sunshine?"

"Rode off into the sunshine," he says.

I'm not over it by the time we get to the airport and join Becky and her parents. I stand off to one side with Becky's father. Don't know what to say. So I say, "I don't think it makes us more bloodthirsty to execute a Charles Manson. I think it's our way of showing that his bloodthirstiness has cost him his right to be considered as a human being. I'd be glad to pull the juice on a serial murderer myself."

Becky's father says, "You're angry. Don't be angry because Dick is leaving home."

I say, "I am not angry because Dick is leaving home. I am angry that he wrecked his car again."

Becky's father says, "I don't know. I think you're angry that he's leaving home."

I hate pop psychology. I go into the men's and try to calm down.

When we say good-bye, I can hardly stand it. It's like I got shot. Like all the stars fall on me. I hold him in my arms for a long time. We rock back and forth. No matter how carefully you prepare for life's great events—like marriage, divorce, a death—when the big thing comes, you are helpless. You can't believe it is really happening. It doesn't help matters much when I suddenly realize that from now on, and forever after, I will just be the past. Dick will return home as long as I live. I hope. But it won't be us living together. It will be him visiting. We will take our old walks, and maybe he will have his baby strapped on his back, the way I had him on mine. The life cycle will go on. But it'll never again be the way it always has been up to now. I think I am going to lose it. I whisper in his ear, "If you knew how much I love you, your socks would fall down." He pulls away and looks at me. He kisses me. Then he and Sydney go through it. Becky's doing the same deal with her parents, and then she calls, *"Richard—let's go!"*

Richard.

How did it happen so fast? At home I'm all out of sorts. Why'd I have to be such a grouch? I wish life came with an eraser on it. I don't remember going into his room—I just find myself sitting at his desk. I look at the scholar-athlete plaque on the wall. I stare at his bed. It's like I got this big sob in me, and I can't let it out. I don't need a drink. Just like you get used to doing it, you can get used to not doing it. A drink won't fix a thing. I haven't missed an AA meeting yet. But it is hardly a force in my life. I finally dared to speak a piece in the meeting, about my pet peeve, giving your problems to God. They jumped in my shit. They said, Oliver, look at what it says in the Twelve Steps. It's God *as we under-stand him.* You don't have to think of God as an old man with a white beard. Think of it as this group. The group is the "Higher Power." Think horizontal, Oliver, not vertical.

So, okay. I want to start being more active. I need to get a sponsor. I can't decide between three oldsters, Al, Harry, or Betty. Al's a sweetheart and Harry's been to the very bottom of things. But Betty is all business. Betty's my man.

Sydney comes in and sits on Dick's bed. She says, "How you doin'?"

I kind of helplessly gesture. Bereft is what I feel.

She says, "Maybe we should go to New York. Not sit here and be sad."

I say, "I don't know about New York."

She goes into the kitchen and calls her father. I can hear the happiness in her voice. Sydney adores her old man. So I guess I got to go down there and face the music. But I don't want to.

I learned my lesson about New York City the first time. I've never been back. When I was just a rookie, I went down there with the chief. We had to pick up a prisoner, a guy who was wanted here for a whole series of bad checks and grand theft auto. Manhattan just awed me—the nuts in the street, the shop windows and sky-scrapers. Country boy goes to the big city. All the differ-ent languages. We had two rooms that connected in this big midtown hotel. We were up there when the chief said, "You know, you ought to go bring that shotgun in out of the car before somebody steals it. We'll hide it under the bed." So I went and got it, and like a dope, I came bopping through the lobby. It was in its scabbard, and I didn't even think; I just went up in the elevator to the room. Not five minutes later there was this *bam bam bam* on the door like to bust the thing down. And in came four uniformed New York City officers. Our guns lay on the bed in their holsters. Their guns were out. The sergeant said, "Who's the stupid fuck that carried that shotgun through the lobby?" I identified myself as the stupid fuck. "Jesus Christ," he said, "don't *ever* do that again." He was not happy. I explained to him that where we live nobody would think a thing about it, certainly not in deer season.

When we went down to the bar, the chief got friendly with a couple of women, laughing and trying to pick them up. I was just a kid, and even though the chief was younger then than I am now, I saw him as an old married man. I was not used to that type of operation. That night we went to a big fancy restaurant with a floor show. Again the chief hooked up with a dolly, he danced with her all night. I was just feeding my face and ogling the chorus girls. We both did a good bit of drinking. Around 1:00 A.M. I was semiwadded, and the chief said he was going home with his newfound friend to her place. He gave me directions for the subway. I didn't pay much attention. Eventually they closed the joint, and I went outside and finally found the subway. I went down, paid my token, and away I went. I rode and rode and rode. I think I dozed off. At last we came to the end of the line.

The guy came through and said everybody had to get off. I was everybody.

I should have got back on the train going the other way, but I went out and figured I'd find a cop and ask him where I was. I had just barely staggered across the street, and I was examining this big empty building when I heard, *"Freeze! Up against the wall!"* I did. He asked for ID, and I said, "I am a police officer from out of town."

He said, "Use your thumb and forefinger, and take it out and drop it in front of you and kick it back to me. Don't turn around."

My badge was in my ID, and I didn't even know for sure he was a cop. I hadn't seen him yet. I was afraid he'd take it, kill me, and go on. But finally it was okay, and I turned around and there was this big huge Irish cop. He said, "OK, Luther," and down the alley there was this black cop crouched with his gun right on me. The Irish cop laughed and said to me, "What the fuck you doing down here?"

I said, "I guess I took the wrong subway."

He said, "Only two kinds of people come here at this hour, pimps and pushers." So he led me like a child back to the subway and told me which train and where to get off. He gave me a free token. When at last I made it back to the hotel room, the chief was in there in bed sound asleep. Either he was a fast worker or it fell through.

I don't want to revisit the scene of my disgrace. And I certainly do not relish the thought of meeting Sydney's father. If he is at all like me, he will strongly disapprove. I'm way too old for his daughter. I sit here at Dick's desk and rehearse a man-to-man talk. I think I will begin by granting him his premise. If Syd and I had kids right now,

I'd be sixty-five when they go off to college. Or Israel. But I don't adore your daughter because I'm middle-aged and she's young. I adore her because she's kind, and beautiful, and smart, and enormous fun to be with. If I were thirty, I'd ask you, sir, for her hand. But if you said no to me, I'd marry her anyway. She's Juliet—she's my Juliet. As things stand now, I know I am not the son-in-law you want. But there's nothing I wouldn't do for her. I can take care of her financially, especially if the chief's job comes through. But she's financially independent anyway. The real question is children. I'm sure that in many ways I have bungled it with Dick, but I can't imagine anything I would trade for the experience of watching him grow up. Biggest thrill of my life. And how, if I truly love her, can I not want her to have that? I mean, children are the one thing that makes me believe God wasn't a complete fool.

I doze off on Dick's bed. An hour later the phone rings, and Syd yells for me to come to it, it's Dick, in Kennedy airport. I wonder what has gone wrong. I am greatly relieved to hear his voice sounding calm and fine. He just wants to check something with me.

He says, "When you take my car to the shop, take that ice-scraper glove out of the trunk."

"Why?" I say.

"Well," he says, "there's something in there, it's right back of the gas tank."

I'm thinking, There's something in there? And then I get it. It's his stash.

He says, "I'm sorry I fucked up, Dad."

I say, "Forget it. I've been sitting at your desk. I already miss you something horrible."

He says, "I've been trying to teach Becky how to play

Pac-Man." He says, "Dad, do you remember how I loved Pac-Man when I was a kid?"

I say, "I remember lots of things about you when you were a kid." I put Sydney on, and I stand here and watch her talk to him. Then I make a signal I want to get on again, and I apologize for being such a grouch.

He says, "No prob."

I realize it's all a blur to him. He's got his eyes on Becky and the whole thing they are doing. It's me who is left behind. Dick is off on the greatest adventure of his life. Dick's not sad. Things are as they should be.

Both Sydney and I are drained. Dick's leaving home is quite a shock to her system, too. She says that when she was his age, she went to college not because she really wanted to, she just went to please her father. She says, "Trips, there are things you don't know about me. Did you know I was busted in high school for keeping dope in my locker? At dinner that night my father said, 'Will the felon please pass the peas?'" She says she did a lot of cocaine in college. Wasted a lot of time. When she met me, she was pretty fucked up in her life.

I think of that guy, her student, and what he did to her.

She says, "My life wasn't productive. I wasn't doing anything. I began to give up on things. I wasn't teaching well."

I say, "But I remember the first time I saw you teach. You did swell."

"Oh," she says, "but I'd already fallen in love with you."

I stare at her. "You had?"

She says in a little wail, "You took *care* of me."

So, now, I hold her and hug her, just as a friend. I rock her.

After a bit, she says, real carefully, "I think . . . I *know* that I want children. Oh, sweetheart—" and she trails off.

I have myself been saying it for so long that I think I have started giving myself credit just for saying it. Mr. Conscientious. But now I see it all in her face. She is scared. It's her life.

I say what I have said so many times before, that I really am too old for her.

"Oh," she says, "maybe you're not too old for me. Maybe I'm too young for you."

That's a big help. Am I going to lose my son and my belovedest on the same day?

She looks at me. "Darling, you really can't see us having kids?"

I don't know. Maybe we could. Maybe. Pretty frightening prospect. I'll do just about anything to hold on to you. But would it be fair to the kid, to have a doddering old fool like me for a father? Jesus. I am an only child. I am the father of an only child. "How big a brood you contemplate having?"

She's been looking at me so seriously, and now my question makes her smile. But she goes on searching my eyes. My heart is pounding just sitting here with her talking about it. Brave is the right way to live. But brave is not foolhardy. Would having kids be brave or foolhardy? I picture myself dandling our baby girl on my knee.

She says, "Last night in the kitchen Dick asked me, 'You gonna marry Dad?' "

I sit up. Now it's my turn, and I just jump into her eyes. "And what did you answer?"

"I said, 'Your Dad hasn't asked me.' "

I drive downtown to the bank, before it closes, and I go in and rummage in my safe-deposit box. I have been thinking about this. I get the ring. My mom gave it to me when she knew she wasn't ever going home again from the hospital. It was her grandmother's. I fumble with the tissue paper. The ring is actually quite simple, gold, with three stones, a ruby flanked by two diamonds. A very plain setting, just prongs around the gems. The ruby is not dull or muddy, it's real clear and bright. It wasn't an engagement ring. Mom's grandfather gave it to her grandmother after all three of their children were born. Three stones for the three girls.

On the way home I get this feeling of dread in my chest. I keep thinking something terrible will happen. Life is going too well. I know I didn't handle it right at the airport, but Dick and I have come out okay. Dick's fine. Except in traffic. Number two, I am beginning to think I actually will get to be chief. I am preparing myself for it, thinking about what my first tasks should be. Three, here she is, Sydney, the most wonderful woman I have ever met. How can things be this good after all the muck and blood and shit of my life? Now I convince myself that I deserve it. If only as a change of pace.

We go out for dinner at the Antlers. We take a long time. We dawdle over our coffee. A big thunderstorm crashes around, and when we go outside, the lush greenery is soaking. But the rain hasn't cooled things off, the temperature and the humidity are both up around ninety. We pull home into the driveway at almost ten, and we see

that my backyard is thronged with fireflies. It's the mois-
ture. They don't just lie low in the grass; it's a firefly
convention. They're all so profuse up in the trees, turning
my whole yard into this swarm of little blinking lights. I
take a blanket out for the damp ground, and we sit by my
little stream. It's this kind of private thicket underneath
my old willow. When you think of fireflies, you think of
them as gold. But they aren't, they are actually a kind of
lime green. We sit on the blanket in the seclusion and
listen to the babble of the stream. We get naked. I am
very eager to make love. But I don't want to rush it. I hear
that men are often unsatisfactory lovers because they
whip through it. I wouldn't know, but it sounds counter-
productive to me. What kind of ninny would want it to
be over? I want it never to be over.

I reach into the pocket of my abandoned pants. I get
the ring in the tissue paper. I am fearful that I am
jumping the gun. She always says I believe in right and
wrong, and I wonder if I am wrong here. She's smoking a
cigarette. She's not supposed to while she's on the pill.
She's got to stop smoking. Or stop the pill. I am befud-
dled. It's so hot, and we are naked as jaybirds.

Well, here goes nothing. I do not get down on one
knee. I get up on one knee. I show her the ring and tell
her the story of it. I say, "The three stones are for the
three girls. One of whom was Grandma. My mother's
mother. She said the big ruby was for her, since she was
the prettiest. Which is why she got the ring."

"And how did your mother get it?"

"Excuse me?"

"You said your mother was one of seven children.
How did she get the ring?"

I realize I don't know. Honey, don't throw me off stride when I am on one knee. And then I see by her voice and in her eyes that she wants to know, because now this ring is hers to wear in her lifetime. She's saying yes. It gets me so flustered I can hardly speak. So I slowly put the ring on her finger. There. We sit on the blanket and watch the fireflies, the whole yard going wild. One little bugger flits down out of the willow trees and goes bing right between us. Syd touches my chest, the ring on her finger. I kiss her cheek, and whisper, "Now we're in trouble."